# Endorsements for *Finding Light in a Lost Year*

One of the few good things to come out of these tough times during the great pandemic of 2020-2022 is a writer willing to be honest about her own experiences and put it on the page in an act of great bravery. Ms. Shulusky has definitely succeeded in her honest and illuminating novel.

–Jonathan Miller
Multi-Award-Winning Mystery Writer
Criminal Defense Lawyer

As we all learn how to adjust our lives during this long, weary pandemic, Carin Fahr Shulusky's newest book, *Finding Light in A Lost Year*, gives readers a sense of encouragement while paying homage to perceived setbacks and big accomplishments that many readers may recognize. This unforgiving pandemic has uprooted all of our lives. As the main character, Roni, narrates the transitions her family endured, readers will learn how Carin's story mirrors so many of our own experiences, challenges, and personal discoveries. *Finding Light in A Lost Year* gives readers a chance to see the difficulties many of us have gone through and to embrace the surprising gifts as well!

–Jill Kraft Thompson
Award-Winning Author of *Finding Jill:*
*How I Rebuilt My Life After Losing the Five People I Loved Most*

*Finding Light in A Lost Year* takes us on one woman's journey through loss, heartbreak, grief and a discovery of what really matters. A page-turning great read.

–Rebecca Now
Founder, Voices of American Herstory

A truly inspiring story about finding oneself in the face of adversity. I loved that it outlined life both before and during the pandemic, and demonstrated the importance of leaning on family and God for support and encouragement—ever ~~in the face of unspeakable~~ tragedy.

~~er~~, MMS, PA-C

D1091946

The proverb says, "The same water that hardens the egg, softens the potato." Difficulties of life test the character of a person, a family, and our relationships. In *Finding Light in A Lost Year,* Carin uses the Covid pandemic to tell a universal story of struggle and survival. No one escapes hardships in life, but as Carin effectively demonstrates, hardships teach lessons that can be learned no other way. Some grow stronger, some succumb, but no one is left unchanged. Like a chick grows stronger breaking free of its shell, Carin demonstrates that families who break free of life's challenges grow stronger, deeper, and richer relationships through perseverance and faith.

–Stephen Hower,
Host, The Hower Hour, Real Talk Radio Network
Author, *Man in the Middle, Sharpening the Sword, Contrary to Popular Belief* and *The Serenity Principles*

A riveting and *true to life* look into one family's journey through the pandemic. The glimmer of hope they held onto was able to shine through as they reworked their lives and strengthened their family bonds.

–Susan Briere,
Library Media Specialist, Dudley, MA

*Finding Light in A Lost Year* is a succinct and colorful story that readers can relate to because the complexities of life during a pandemic affected all of us in some similar ways. Shulusky does a beautiful job while telling an interesting fictional story weaving the good news of what is most important in life. The prayer offered at the end sums up the lessons of this tale perfectly. This will be a valuable book in future years as we try to describe to younger generations what the years of the pandemic were like here in America. More importantly, it will show that God cares deeply about each one of us and will use whatever He has (even a pandemic) to bring His beloved children closer to Him.

–Susan Bentzinger
CrossWalk Bookstore

Carin Shulusky's latest endeavor, *Finding Light in A Lost Year*, is an absolute gem, a faith based mix of fact and fiction, a cautionary tale about the seemingly perfect upwardly mobile Wright family told in the first person in chronicle form through the point of view of Roni, the family's matriarch.

Readers will laugh and cry and want to shake a character or two as this family traverses a global pandemic, career obstacles, personal tragedies and triumphs. A real stand out in this novel is the realistic perspective of just how difficult it has been to navigate the pandemic for families with children—from no school to virtual learning—and finally back in the classroom, plus the plethora of good and bad newsworthy things that happened in the states and around the world during 2020 and 2021.

With an even paced and easy to understand dialogue, and an interesting cast of characters dealing with real life conflicts, this little treasure will appeal to a range of readers, including fans of women's fiction and inspirational fiction.

Roni Wright had it all: a globe-trotting successful executive for a travel company, married to her handsome architect husband Nathan, a young daughter, Katlin, and her young son Oliver. Then, a global pandemic struck and suddenly both children had no school to go to, Nathan's office closed but he now has more work than ever, which leaves him floundering about where in this abruptly noisy house to set up shop. And, lastly, there's no more travel so no more travel industry, leaving Roni, a fish out of water, in charge of everything at home but feeling incapable of handling anything at all. But that's just the tip of the iceberg when some well-kept secrets come to light, threatening the very foundation of this suddenly very imperfect family.

–Debbie Haupt, Blogger
The Reading Frenzy

# finding
# light in a
# lost
# year

## Carin Fahr Shulusky

Fossil Creek Press

**Finding Light in a Lost Year**
Carin Fahr Shulusky
Fossil Creek Press

Published by Fossil Creek Press, St. Louis, MO
Copyright ©2022 Carin Fahr Shulusky
All rights reserved.

Editors: Carol Corley and Karen Tucker

Cover illustrator: Janice Schoultz Mudd

Cover and Interior design: Davis Creative Publishing Partners, CreativePublishingPartners.com

Publisher's Cataloging-In-Publication Data
Names: Shulusky, Carin Fahr, author.
Title: Finding light in a lost year / Carin Fahr Shulusky.
Description: St. Louis, MO : Fossil Creek Press, [2021]
Identifiers: ISBN 9781736241721 (paperback) | ISBN 9781736241738 (ebook)
Subjects: LCSH: COVID-19 (Disease)--Social aspects--Fiction. | Families--Fiction. | Loss (Psychology)--Fiction. | Faith--Fiction. | LCGFT: Domestic fiction. | Christian fiction. | BISAC: FICTION / Family Life / General. | FICTION / Family Life / Siblings.
Classification: LCC PS3619.H855 M9 2022 (print) | LCC PS3619.H855 (ebook) | DDC 813/.6--dc23

LCCN: 2021924517

*I'd like to dedicate this book to the remarkably brave health care warriors who fought for us all on the front lines of the 2020 pandemic. Whether in hospitals, nursing homes, clinics, or ambulances, they sacrificed so much to keep us safe, heal the sick, and comfort those who couldn't be saved. Many gave the ultimate sacrifice. They are the heroes of the pandemic.*
*Thank you.*

# Acknowledgments

I'd first like to acknowledge my two wonderful editors. My dear friend Carol Corley is my sounding board for everything I think and write. She is my greatest cheerleader and best critic. She makes everything I write better. Second is my marvelous editor Karen Tucker. She carefully took a raw manuscript and made it sparkle. She made the process more fun than it should be.

I'd like to also thank my dear family. My husband Richard is the man who truly knows the best recording of Mozart's *The Magic Flute,* the origins of the Blues, and the history of the Peloponnesian War. My brilliant daughter Christine Blonn, her amazing husband Phil, their delightfully effervescent daughter Sophie, and my always humorous son Andy are the brightest lights of my life. They giving my life meaning and purpose

# Table of Contents

*Your word is a lamp to my feet*
*and a light for my path.*
Psalm 119:105 (NIV)


*When Jesus spoke again to the people he*
*said, "I am the light of the world. Whoever*
*follows me will never walk in darkness, but*
*will have the light of life."*
John 8:12 (NIV)


*"For I know the plans I have for you,"*
*declares the Lord, "plans to prosper you and*
*not to harm you, plans to give you hope and*
*a future. Then you will call on me and come*
*and pray to me, and I will listen to you. You*
*will seek me and find me when you seek me*
*with all your heart."*
Jeremiah 29:11-13 (NIV)

# Prologue

Do you remember where you were on Thanksgiving of 2019? Do you remember how you celebrated that happy year? And with whom? My guess is a rather large group of family and friends from parts far and wide. Do you remember how you were feeling about the future? I do. I remember it all. I felt on top of the world. It was a time of plenty. Plenty of everything. There was never a gap on any store shelf. Anything and everything you wanted was right at your fingertips. If you wanted to go somewhere, you hopped on a plane and went. No restrictions. Life was rich, full, and glorious, or so I thought. I truly had it all. My name is Veronica (I prefer Roni) Krieger Wright. I've been married for twelve years to my handsome, successful architect husband, Nathan. (I also sort of have a boyfriend, but that's another story). We have two perfect, brilliant, happy children (one boy and one girl, of course)—Oliver and Katlin. My husband and I had sound, successful careers, and our world couldn't have been more perfect, or so I thought. I couldn't have been more wrong. How could we know that a worldwide pandemic was lurking just around the corner, threatening to take it all away? This is the story of that pandemic and how it exposed the vast imperfections in my perfect world, how we nearly lost everything that mattered, and how we not only survived My Lost Year, but also how we found what truly mattered in the wake of the worst pandemic in a hundred years.

# November 2019 – A Perfect World

Sometimes the trip from Winnetka, Illinois, to St. Louis felt like it took days. It usually took just under six hours, depending on the weather and how many times the kids needed to stop. This time, it seemed like an eternity.

Nathan and I and our two children were on our way home from celebrating Thanksgiving with my in-laws. We made the trek to Winnetka about three times a year. This year, Nathan's family got Thanksgiving. Next year, they'll get Christmas. I was already dreading that. We left St. Louis last Wednesday. Now, after completing all the family obligations, we were headed home.

Our Thanksgiving was great, if you don't count the fact that my five-year-old son Oliver broke an antique vase at my in-laws or that my seven-year-old daughter Katlin threw up in our Cadillac Escalade one hour into the trip. Overall, as trips to my snobby in-laws go, it was successful. We had an elegant Thanksgiving dinner at their club. My children made only minor distractions. I had bribed them for good behavior with the promise of a new toy for the trip home. It was now occupying them in the back seat. Of course, they each had their own iPad with earphones too, which should have helped reduce the squabbling. *Should have.* With two more hours to go of the drive, I resorted to threats.

"I will take away those iPads and you won't have any screen time for a whole week if you don't stop arguing right now," I screamed, for effect. I could control my temper if I really wanted to. *Please, God, make them*

3

*be good.* I couldn't possibly handle a whole week without the distraction of iPads.

Fortunately, quiet ensued, and I didn't have to find out how far my resolve would go. With that settled, I was back to my own iPad, setting up appointments with clients for the coming week. I had barely looked at my phone over the holiday. I did have that conference call with Boeing on Wednesday as we drove down. And I spent a couple of hours Friday working on a holiday tour. I was the manager of the St. Louis office of Jonas Travel and Events, a worldwide business and incentive travel agency. Five years ago, after Oliver was born, I had convinced them to open an office in St. Louis. At the time, Nathan was being transferred to St. Louis with his firm. We both thought we could prosper in St. Louis and raise our family there. My parents live in nearby Washington, Missouri, and I knew I could count on them to help out with the kids. It had worked pretty well so far. I had no idea what the next year, 2020, would hold for us. At this moment, we seemed to be on top of the world, if only I could get these kids to stop bickering.

"Alright, hand me those iPads right now," I said much more firmly than I meant.

"OK, Mom. We'll stop," Katlin and Oliver replied in unison. Lucky for me. I really had no plan to take those electronic babysitters away.

"I suppose we should stop for dinner," Nathan said, reminding me that there was another parent in the car.

"How about Springfield?" I replied. "We'll need a pretty quick meal. We have to get home and get these two in bed. Tomorrow is school for them and work for us."

"I'm pretty exhausted," Nathan said. "But we'll find a chain restaurant that won't take long." So that's what we did.

Bright and early the next day, our crazy morning rush began again. There was something strangely comforting and familiar about our routine. Everyone was up at 6. I faithfully went to the gym Monday, Wednesday, and Friday before work. I dropped the kids off at school for the Early Bird program at 7 a.m. before heading to the gym for my workout. Nathan liked to be in his office early, so he would go straight to work. We took turns dropping off the kids at 8 a.m. on Tuesday and Thursday. Nathan worked out after work on some days. I wasn't sure what he did the other days. Our nanny, Anna, picked up the kids after school. She was a lifesaver. I had met her on one of my trips to Germany. She was taking classes at Washington University while working for us. It was a perfect arrangement. She was teaching the kids German too.

As I said, our life was pretty perfect. If either or both of us had to work late, we knew Anna would be there. I always had frozen meals on hand, and Anna had a credit card to get pizza or whatever delivered. Everything ran like clockwork in our perfect world.

My day began with a tough workout with Grace, my personal trainer and friend. She's been training me ever since we moved to St. Louis. She not only helped me stay in shape, but she was somewhat of a mother confessor too. She knew all my darkest secrets, which I must admit numbered too many. It always cheered me to see her.

"So, how was the big Thanksgiving with your in-laws?" Grace asked as she programmed the treadmill to take me up hills a little faster than I like.

"It all went smoothly," I answered, breathing hard. "Oliver did break one of my mother-in-law's prize vases, but I don't count that."

"Still not a fan of Nathan's mother, then?" she asked.

"Oh, I don't think I'll ever…be…a…fan," I gasped as the treadmill pushed me to my limits. "She's such a society matron. Totally dedicated to her clubs and causes," I added when the torture machine had stopped. "She's much more interested in her latest hairdo than her grandkids."

"Roni, is that really fair? She loves your kids," Grace countered.

"Oh, she loves showing them off at her club, I suppose. Especially when they're perfectly 'turned out,' as she would say, in clothes she purchased. Is that really love?" I asked, once again breathing hard as I lifted weights.

"I imagine in her world it is," she answered.

"Well, she's not a fan of my world," I said, panting. "She's always asking pointed questions about how much time I spend at work and how the kids are doing in their studies, like I should know everything."

Grace didn't respond. I suppose she didn't exactly approve of my life either. She had reason. She knew it all. But we remained close because she doesn't judge. After all, she's been in and out of relationships so often, I've lost count.

Back in the locker room, we continued our conversation as I dressed for work. "The big question is, did you see *him* while you were in Chicago?" Grace asked.

I couldn't pretend I didn't know whom she meant. While I had been living and working in Chicago, I had developed a rather too-close relationship with the manager of our Chicago office, Dan Phillips. I had hoped to see Dan on our trip, but family obligations never left any room. It didn't matter. There would be upcoming trips together. Honestly, I wasn't sure if I wanted to continue our… whatever it was. Best to keep our "friendship" on a professional level.

"No, I didn't," I said coolly. "That would have been totally inappropriate. Besides, you know I never mix business and family."

"Oh, well, as long as you're being appropriate," she said smiling. I snapped the towel at her, and we both laughed.

"Seriously, Grace, I know I have to stop this 'thing,' whatever it is. I love Nathan, and I wouldn't want to hurt him for the world."

"But, do you think you can resist him while you're both in Germany?" she asked.

"Oh, God, I wish I could. He makes me feel—I don't know—noticed, beautiful, sexy? And those blue eyes of his…I just get lost. It's like a disease."

"I think more like a moth drawn to the flame," she said.

"An apt description. Should something happen, I swear it will be the last time," I vowed.

When I arrived in my office, I was pleased to see my staff hard at work. We mostly arranged corporate group travel, meetings, and incentive travel. We've done everything from arranging travel and entertainment to conducting small or large meetings. Our biggest earner were incentive or rewards trips that major companies give to top sales reps or clients. Since I'm fluent in German and Japanese and I know some Italian, I often supervised those trips "on the ground," as we say.

We were planning a big tour to Germany, Austria, and Switzerland just before Christmas. It was one of my favorite trips. Our client for this trip was a major pharmaceutical company, who used it to reward their top sales reps. I called it the Christmas Market Tour. That's how it was promoted to the reps. The cost was astronomical, but this pharmaceutical company got a lot of mileage from their reps with this "carrot." The Christmas markets in those countries had become a major draw, and Jonas has cashed in on the trend. This client was very important, and I went along to make sure all details were in place. It gave the client an extra measure of security knowing a manager was on site with them. There were many details to settle before we left. I'd be gone from December 5 to the 12.

My office was set up in threes. Three account managers, three business managers, and three support staff, or clerical people. I was the boss, but I had a couple of key accounts, the pharmaceutical company being the main one. Boeing sort of fell in my lap. My brother Adam worked at Boeing, and they were looking to outsource some of their corporate group travel. They had some big military accounts in Asia, including in Japan, so they liked my ability to speak Japanese. I worked a few times as a translator for them when they had difficulties in discussions with the Japanese. It's a service I was glad to offer for this lucrative account.

As it was Monday morning, we all gathered for our weekly staff meeting. As the staff members were taking their seats, I noticed a new face. I had nearly forgotten that we had recently replaced one of our personal assistants who was on maternity leave.

"We have a new member of our team today," I said, quickly gathering all the pieces in my head. "Let me introduce Susan Krupp, personal assistant, who will be filling in for Jennifer while she's on maternity leave. Perhaps it would help Susan if I introduced our staff. On my right is Kari Knight, account manager. Her biggest account is Enterprise. Next to Kari is Clark York, account manager. He handles Anheuser-Busch InBev, and next to him is Andrew Upchurch, who works with Washington University, among others. At the far end is Abigail Lindwood, our accountant. Next to her is Gavin Seiberg, who handles everything IT. Catherine Burke is next. She's our events coordinator. I think you've already met our office manager, Megan Arft. Megan works mostly for me but also anyone else who needs help. Sarah Linn is the other personal assistant. She mainly assists the account managers. You are our wild card, as it were. You will help wherever it's needed. Megan can help you sort out who needs what. I'm sure you'll get to know all of us soon. We're a pretty close-knit family here. Do you have any questions, Susan?"

Poor Susan. I'd really put her on the spot. She looked like the proverbial deer in the headlights. "Not just now," she said softly. "That's a lot to learn."

"Well, I'm sure you'll pick it up fast. We'll all help, won't we, team?"

My question was answered by murmurs all around, a little less enthusiastic than I would have liked. "Alright. For this week's challenges: Catherine will be working out all the details of the Christmas Market Tour with our New York office. I will also be working on the January Japan trip with Boeing executives. I'll need Catherine and Megan on this," I finished, drawing a deep breath. "Kari, your turn. What's up with your accounts this week?"

As I sat at the head of our highly polished conference table, I couldn't help but feel satisfied. We were a good team—no, a great team. I loved these people. I had made it my priority to know them personally. I loved what we did, and we were good at it. *Yes, life is good,* I thought. *Just about perfect. I must confess, I love being the boss.*

Later that day, Catherine and Megan were in my office going over some details of the upcoming trips.

"This Christmas Market Tour is going to make your family Christmas plans difficult, I suppose," Megan said thoughtfully. "I'd be happy to help any way I can."

"That's so kind of you, Megan." I smiled. "I'm sure I'll manage. I may take advantage of the Christmas markets myself. I've hired a designer to decorate my house, inside and out, so I don't have to put much effort into Christmas. I'm sure Nathan will help out." I paused for a thoughtful moment and added, "I hope Nathan will help out."

"Well, you let me know if there's anything I can do to help," she offered. "I'm sure Nathan will be glad for my help."

"One thing you could help with is the Jonas Christmas party," I told her. "I want to go all out this year. I'd like to have it at my house. I want to make good use of our grand old house in Willow Glen. But we'll need caterers. Something elegant; not just the usual fare. And we should have a bartender and music. Oh, and valet parking. I want lots of holiday flowers too. We should invite some clients. Ask the account people who they want to invite. Probably should hold the line at fifty people. That means it will need to be more of an open house, with a buffet. We manage corporate events, so we should show them how well we can throw a party," I added with a great deal of pride.

"Of course," Megan said. "I'll take care of all the details. Just leave it to me."

*How sweet she is. We all get along so well. Yes, life is pretty perfect.*

# December 2019 –
# Glamorous Holiday

The days flew by. Soon it was time for my trip to Europe and the Christmas Market Tour. We had thirty people signed on to take this tour. It may not seem like a big number for a land tour, but it's plenty. Dan Phillips was also bringing thirty people from Chicago. We would rotate the venues but mostly be in the same cities at the same time. I wasn't completely sure how I felt about this. Dan and I had some very romantic—or, at least, torrid—times together while traveling, depending on how you look at it. We were both married and have no plans to change that status. I thought Dan was always a shoulder to cry on when things weren't going too well with Nathan. But now Nathan and I had so much to lose. I knew Dan would just laugh that lovely deep laugh of his and say, "Isn't that what makes this so safe, darling? We both have so much to lose." I was so weak when he was around. I knew the right thing to do, but I couldn't seem to do the right thing. It is the thing I didn't want to do that I always ended up doing. *What's wrong with me?*

Just thinking of Dan made me throw that sexy black lace chemise in the suitcase as I packed. *I really have to stop. This is not who I want to be.* I grabbed the chemise and threw it back in the drawer. *I can be a better wife. I know I can.*

As usual when I'm gone for any length of time, my mother was coming to manage the house. Washington is a lovely little town on the banks of the Missouri River, about an hour's drive from where we live in Willow Glen. It didn't hold much for me, but I understood why my parents stayed there. My dad was a family doctor. He had a small practice and worked part-time at Mercy Hospital, the only Level III Trauma Center between St. Louis and Jefferson City. He'd been affiliated with them since I was a small child. Washington suited them. I think they originally moved there because of its German connection. It looks like a town on the Rhine. They both have German parents, and they liked the connection. I suspect they stayed because the lifestyle was slow and easy. Just their pace. I heard their car pulling up to our house, closed the suitcase, and went downstairs to meet them.

"Grandma, Grandpa," my kids were squealing. They openly loved my parents, and the feelings were warmly returned. Hugs were administered all around.

"Hello, Mom," I said. "I'm so glad to see you. You too, Dad."

"I suppose I get second billing because I'm not the person giving up a week to stay with your kids," he said, smiling.

"Now, Robert, be nice," my mother admonished with a smile. "He's just put out because he can't stay. He has to be at the hospital tomorrow."

"And I'll miss her terribly," Dad added. "I wish we could just pack these cuties in the car and take them back to Washington. A little country air would do them good."

"Can we? Can we?" Katlin and Oliver cried in unison.

"You know you have school tomorrow," I said sternly.

"Oh, Mom, please," Katlin wailed. "You know I don't like school this year. I'm sure no one would miss me if I was gone a few days."

"I hardly think it works like that, but good try." I laughed, a little puzzled.

"What if I come back Friday and pick them up for the weekend?" Dad asked.

"I'll have to check with Nathan," I said. "They do have two parents." I wondered for a moment, *do they have two parents?* Sometimes I felt like I was in this alone. Nathan was supposed to be home an hour ago.

He knew I had to get ready for my trip. *Couldn't he just once be on time? Why doesn't he ever support my work?*

Just then, the "other parent" came in the room. He apologized to my parents for being late. He didn't apologize to me.

"Please, Dad!" Oliver and Katlin begged. "Can we go to Grandma and Grandpa's for the weekend?"

"I don't see why not," he answered. "But let me drive at least one way."

"OK," said Dad. "I'll pick them up right after school on Friday, and you can come get them Sunday, whenever you want. Just don't make it too early," he added.

"Fair enough," Nathan said. "I'll text you when I'm ready to leave Sunday. I have a lot of work to do this week, and this will help."

"Where's that nanny of yours?" Mom asked.

"I'm here," said Anna, walking into the room. She had a rather uncanny habit of popping up unexpectedly. It was almost like she'd been hiding until her name was mentioned.

"We'll have to go through schedules and activities with my mom," I told her. "But we have good news. You'll get next weekend off because my parents are taking the kids to Washington after school Friday."

"That's wunderbar," Anna exclaimed, lapsing into her German. "I have so much school work. It will give me time to catch up."

"I don't know why you need Anna while I'm here," Mom said. "I think I can take care of two little darlings myself."

"I'm sure you can, Mom, but Anna knows our routine and she can help with driving. Both Katlin and Oliver have ice skating lessons, and Katlin has her Girl Scout meeting. Anna will be a big help with all that." This was a common theme with my mom. She never approved of a nanny, and I thought she wanted to prove I didn't need her.

Just then, Katlin ran back into the room. "Make sure Grandma knows I have to have my Burberry shoes you promised for school. All the girls have them, and I can't show up without Burberry shoes." I suddenly remembered how Katlin had been stressing over the right shoes and clothes for school.

"Katlin, I'll order them online right now and they'll be here in a few days. This isn't something Grandma or Anna needs to worry about just now. I promise to take care of it."

"Alright, if you promise," Katlin said, a little too snarkily, and stomped off.

"I can see there are issues here I might need help with. I suppose Anna and I can team up," Mom conceded. I was growing more concerned about Katlin's school problems. If only I didn't have to leave right now, but my job was too important. How else would I afford those Burberry shoes?

"I think it's time for me to go," Dad chimed in. "I have a long, lonely drive home."

"Why not stay for supper?" I asked. "We can get that pizza you like."

"No, I'd better start for home. But I'll see you two monkeys on Friday," he said, poking each grandchild in the stomach and laughing.

We all hugged, and Dad left. There was a lot to do before bed, and I had an early flight. I was exhausted as I flopped into bed hoping for a few hours of sleep. Nathan flopped rather loudly next to me.

"How about some fun before you leave?" he asked, rubbing my thigh. *Really? Now? Where was he when I was ordering the right shoes for Katlin or paying the bills or going over the kids' schedules? Where was he then?*

"Not now, I'm exhausted," I replied, pushing his hand away.

Before I knew it, I was on a plane headed for Munich. It was good to just sit and think. *Life is such a whirlwind,* I thought. I wasn't worried about the tour. I had every confidence in our ground suppliers for guides. They didn't need me. Most spoke excellent English, but I knew my presence would show our client how special they were. It was important that I ensured this big client was happy. We had carefully planned nearly every moment. But things always happen. A client could lose a passport or luggage or become ill. I was trained to handle almost anything, and it had all happened one time or another. I studied the list of guests in my group. It was important to know each of their names and where they were from. The more personal I could be, the happier they would be. I was meeting Dan in Munich to go over our schedules. My mind drifted back to his deadly blue eyes and that wicked smile. Soon, I drifted off to sleep.

I must have been very tired because we were already flying over the ocean when I woke up. The stewardess was offering me a meal. I couldn't even think what meal I should be eating. It didn't matter much. Airline food was airline food. On the way home, I would fly Lufthansa. Their food was always worth waking up for. After the meal, I found a movie to watch, and by the time that was over, we were ready to land in Munich. I loved this city. Its historical elegance always thrilled me. Once, before kids, I had hoped I could find a way to live there, but that never worked out. The Germans don't need interpreters. Most of them speak at least some English.

As I entered my hotel, Dan was there waiting. He must have been thinking the same things I had been thinking about. He greeted me with a warm hug and a big smile.

"I'm so glad we could do this tour together," he said. "You look so tired, my beautiful friend. I think you need some pampering. You work much too hard."

"Yes, but it's my job. This tour is pretty grueling. I had a lot to do to get ready for this trip." I sighed.

"I bet you've been doing all the work alone, my poor sweet. I wish I could whisk you away to some sunny location. However, we'll just have to make the most of the time we have." He smiled back. Oh, that smile. Those sparkling eyes. I could resist anything but that smile and those eyes. He seemed to really care about me. "Let's get our work done and have some playtime tonight, OK?"

*Run, run,* my mind was saying. No more "playtime." But that wasn't my answer. "Of course. I can't wait to catch up."

We went to the Hofbrau Haus for dinner. It's always such fun. Even though I would be taking my group there, it was nice to share it with Dan. The beer was so good. So much beer! Then we went back to my room and caught up—much too much. It was so nice to be with a man without having to worry about the kids down the hall or the dirty wash that needed cleaning or the bills that needed paying or the one hundred and one other tasks that had to be done. We didn't argue about how quickly Katlin was becoming besties with the wrong girls or how slowly Oliver was learning to read. It was just two people enjoying each other without a worry in the world. Life was so perfect. But when I woke the next morning, Dan was gone, and I felt stupid. I picked up my phone and saw a message from Nathan. It said, "I hope you're having a good trip. Miss you. Love you." I felt more miserable than I had ever felt. What had I done? The guilt overwhelmed me. I knew in that moment that I would never, ever do that again.

That morning, our guests started arriving. I was on the clock from that point to the end of the tour. Although I passed Dan from time to time, we didn't have any more alone time. The trip went very smoothly, due mostly to our superb planning and good weather and our excellent local destination management company that had ironed out all the details. We had a little snow at just the right moments but never too much. The only wrinkle came when we lost one guest and had one hysterical husband for a short time during free-time shopping in Oberammergau.

"Mrs. Wright, I've lost my wife!" screamed a frantic husband.

"Mr. Hill, we never lose anyone. Just misplace them for a while," I told him as calmly as possible. It was a firm policy at Jonas Travel that we never use the word "lost," only "misplaced." I usually found that wording comforting. "Now tell me, where did you see her last?"

"We were shopping in one of those Hummel places, and she said she was going next door to look. When I came out, I couldn't find her. Now it's time to get on the bus and she's lost," he said with big tears in his eyes. I wondered if Nathan would be so upset if I were missing.

"I'm sure the only thing she has lost is the time," I told him, trying hard to be sympathetic. Mrs. Hill was one of those tourists who was intent on buying out every city she entered. I suspected we hadn't allowed nearly enough time for her to complete all her purchases.

I knew Dan's group was still in the shops, so I texted him to look for Mrs. Hill. He found her in short order, and I went to collect the errant guest. As I approached Mrs. Hill, I saw Dan with his arms wrapped around one of his clients, whispering in her ear. As she moved away, he gave her a little pat on the bottom. She turned and gave him a wicked smile. I knew in that moment Dan was not the charming man I thought him to be. He was a fiend, not a friend. I would have nothing more to do with Dan Phillips. He was out of my life.

We were delayed only 30 minutes from our departure from Oberammergau. Not bad for a "misplaced" person. Not surprisingly, Mrs. Hill was not in the least bit remorseful. She only regretted not making more purchases. I kept a closer eye on her the rest of the trip. Our local guide knew so many of the shopkeepers, he could alert them to her interests, and they helped her buy as much as her heart desired within the allotted time. A win for everyone. I had even prepared a plan for the extra luggage I knew she would end up with.

In spite of the hectic pace, I managed to buy a few gifts myself. I got a lovely hand-carved wooden doll for Katlin that had a music box inside and twirled when it played and a wooden train for Oliver. After the last guest was safely on the way home, I boarded my flight totally exhausted. I had a restful trip home, enjoying the Lufthansa meals and dreaming of how delighted my kids would be with the German gifts.

There was little time for jet lag when I returned. Christmas was a little over two weeks away. Our big Christmas party was scheduled for December 18—it was as close to Christmas as I could get without losing people to holiday travel. Unfortunately, it was a school night, so I had arranged for Anna to spend the night and keep the kids upstairs.

Megan had hired a cleaning crew of four to give the house a thorough cleaning. This was beyond my regular cleaning lady's ability. Glenda Field had cleaned for us for nearly four years. She was good, but I needed our house to sparkle for the big party. I gave her the job of field marshal for the two days of cleaning. She relished the post, and the end result was amazing. Our dear old house never looked so good.

We lived in Willow Glen, a lovely old suburb of St. Louis. Most of the houses here were close to 100 years old, some even older. Our house was built in 1929 by a man who owned several factories in the area. It had four bedrooms and a "maid's quarter" off the kitchen that was mostly used for storage. The star feature of our house is the spectacular two-and-a-half-story foyer that leads to a grand staircase. On one side of the foyer is the lush dining room, and on the other side is a large sunken living room. One wall of the living room has floor-to-ceiling windows. On the far side of the living room is a smaller family room where we spend most of our time. I had filled the house with treasures from my travels: a colorful rug from India, baskets from Botswana, masks from Nepal, beautiful steins of every style from Germany, and Hummels everywhere.

The party would move from the living room to the dining room. We removed most of the chairs and extraneous furniture from the dining room to increase the standing room. The staircase was covered in evergreen garland with red bows and gold accents. A 10-foot fresh-cut Christmas tree decorated (by a florist) to match the garland stood in the curved window just inside the living room. A stunning Hummel nativity sat at the base of the tree. The effect was stunning, if I do say so myself, although I had done none of the decorating. But I'm a manager, not a doer.

The day of the party came quickly. When the caterers arrived, they took over the house. Nathan picked up McDonald's Happy Meals for the kids. So, they were…happy. I had found a lovely cocktail dress in red and gold to match the decorations. A bar had been set up in the foyer. It was time for me to play hostess. I had thirty-five positive responses to my invitation, among them some of our best clients. This included my brother Adam, who was one of my contacts at Boeing, and his girlfriend Melissa. She looked gorgeous in blue velvet. Everyone from the office was there with a significant other.

"Everything is amazing. You certainly know how to throw a party," Megan said with a bit of a smirk. We both knew she did most of the work.

"I couldn't have done it without you," I replied. "I understand you finalized a lot of the plans with Nathan while I was away. I'm so grateful for all your help. The caterers you found are perfect, and the flow plan is working wonderfully. Thank you so much," I gushed. I gave her a big hug as she colored a deep red. I supposed she wasn't used to getting compliments. I made a mental note to do it more often.

Nathan slipped in next to me and put an arm around my waist. "You've done well, my dear," he said. "Of course, I never doubted. Grand gestures are your signature." Again, Megan blushed. I suppose she's not used to anyone getting compliments.

The evening was a huge success. As I slid into bed that night next to Nathan, I marveled at how well this girl from Washington, Missouri, had done. All had been perfect.

My next big hurtle was Christmas. I had invited my parents to come and stay for a few days. I had also invited my Aunt Mary and Uncle Stan for Christmas Day dinner. Their kids were all visiting in-laws Christmas Day. She's my mother's sister, and we've always enjoyed having them around. Also coming were my sister Korie with her husband Geoff and their two boys, Henry and James. Adam and Melissa will be there as well. We'd also invited Nathan's younger brother Collin and his girlfriend Stefanie. She lived in St. Louis, and Collin was already in town visiting.

That made twelve adults and four children for Christmas dinner. No problem. My mother would cook everything. She's so good in the kitchen, why would I even try? At least I would buy all the groceries. She texted me her grocery list, which I promptly gave to Nathan. Everything was ready for a wonderful Christmas. The prime rib cost a small fortune, but it's Christmas.

"Do you have any idea how much that prime rib cost?" Nathan said, half furious and half exasperated. "I think I could buy a small car for less. I just spent $600 on groceries. GROCERIES!" he shouted.

"I know it's expensive, but it's Christmas," I replied. "Don't we deserve something a little special this time of year?"

"I don't know about that, but I don't think we deserve to go broke by January. Have you finished buying all the Christmas presents? What about the kids' Santa lists? Have you picked up all that?" he asked.

"I have some lovely gifts for the kids," I replied, a little hurt. "I didn't check the Santa lists, but what I have is so much better. I'm sure they'll be delighted."

"Are you sure of that?" he challenged. "Will they be as delighted as my family was with all their Japanese kimonos?" He actually smirked.

"They loved those kimonos. You can't buy them here. They're antique. Very unique," I said defensively.

"Just make sure there is something under that enormous Christmas tree our kids actually want," he demanded. *Of course, he could check lists, buy the gifts, and wrap them,* I thought. *I'm not the only parent.*

Now I was a little worried. This could be a chink in my fabulous Christmas plans. I scurried to find the Santa letters. When my search failed to turn up even a trace, I called my mother.

"Mom, did you take the kids to see Santa?" I asked.

"Yes, I did, sweetie," she said. "We had a wonderful visit. Didn't you see the pictures I left you? Why do you ask?"

"Well, I was wondering if you know what they asked Santa for," I said a little sheepishly.

"It's three days before Christmas and you don't have any idea what your kids want for Christmas?" she said way too smugly.

"I've been a little distracted," I told her. "I bought some lovely toys in Germany," I added with an air of confidence.

"Toys they really want?" Really, this was becoming a common theme. Do both my husband and my mom think I'm a terrible mother?

"I'm sure they'll love them. I just thought we should have something from their Santa lists too."

"I was pretty sure you hadn't seen the lists, so I purchased some things they requested. I know you have a busy life, but their happiness is very important. I got the impression all the girls in Katlin's class are getting American Girl dolls. If she doesn't get a specific one, she'll be— oh, what did she say?—uncool."

"I'm very grateful, Mom. Sounds like you may have saved the day. I'll repay you. I suppose I should have paid more attention. I've just been so busy. I do want them to have a good Christmas." My mother always had a way of making me feel just as ashamed as she intended, without actually criticizing me. She was brilliant. I've never managed her level of parenting.

"We're coming down first thing on the twenty-third, so I'll have plenty of time to cook," she added a little too pointedly. "Have you found a place for us to attend Christmas Eve services?" My mother was probably the most devout Christian I knew. Actually, most of my acquaintances weren't Christian at all. Nathan and I identified as Christian but rarely attended services.

"I'll get on that right away," I promised. "Since you are doing so much cooking for Christmas, Nathan and I will take the family out to dinner on Christmas Eve."

"That would be lovely," Mom replied.

I had a full day of work, but now I had to find a Presbyterian church with an early service and dinner reservations. That proved much more difficult, since so many places were closed for Christmas Eve, and I'd waited way too late to make reservations. After I struck out several times trying to find both, I put Megan on the task. It's not her responsibility, but I was desperate. She found a church service at 4 p.m. at an elegant church nearby. It was the children's service, which I thought would be better for the kids.

"I could get you a reservation at Chaucer's Steak House for 5:30 p.m.," Megan told me. "Do you think Nathan would like that?"

"Nathan will be fine with whatever we get," I said, a little puzzled about her concern with what Nathan likes. After all, *I'm* her boss. "But Chaucer's is awfully expensive, and it's not very kid friendly."

"Well, most places only have reservations at 4:30 or 9," Megan told me. "I don't see how either of those times would work. I only got the reservations at Chaucer's because we've held events there. They're fitting you in as a favor."

"O.K. Chaucer's it is." I didn't think Nathan would be at all happy about the cost, but I wasn't going to share that with Megan—she seemed much too interested in Nathan's opinion.

Christmas came and went as it always did. The church service was lovely, although the kids squirmed throughout the service. You'd think they'd never been to church before. Well, they hadn't much. We probably wouldn't have gone Christmas Eve, but my mother insisted. My mother was resplendent in a shimmering red sweater and black velvet skirt. She even had a red and green crystal necklace. She does love Christmas. My kids were pretty well turned out, especially since my mother had bought them each something dressy to wear. Chaucer's was, as I expected, astronomically expensive. I think they must boost prices Christmas Eve. They made hamburgers for the kids, but they each spilled something, and Oliver broke a saltshaker. I wouldn't have thought it possible to break a saltshaker. Leave it to Oliver.

On Christmas morning, my lovely gifts from Germany were soon shoved to the side for the American Girl doll and mechanical dinosaur my mother had bought. I would have to thank her again. Dinner was fabulous, but the Christmas cake I ordered from one of my favorite pastry shops in Munich was not well received. No, that's an understatement. Oliver actually spit it out. I wanted to reprimand him, but Nathan spit his out too. He did it much more politely, but I got the general idea. Fortunately, we had ice cream on hand.

My parents stayed for a couple of days because Nathan and I both had to go to work right after Christmas and I wanted to give Anna a little Christmas break. My parents once again proved to be much better grandparents than we were parents by taking the kids ice skating at Steinberg Rink, a St. Louis tradition. They also had a fun day at the Science Center and Magic House, neither of which I had been to with the kids. *I must do better.* I made it my first New Year's resolution: Spend more time with the kids. But on the whole, life just couldn't get any better. It was just perfect.

# January 2020 –
# Ringing in the Perfect Year

"Hurray! It's 2020!" I shouted. I loved the sound of 2020. It's so symmetrical. So perfect.

"Happy New Year!" I added to no one in particular as confetti was falling from the ceiling. A bottle of good champagne may have added to my mood, but it was a wonderful party. I quickly found Nathan in the crowd and grabbed him for my New Year's kiss. It was a very good kiss too. I had to admit I looked rather dazzling. I chose a long slim silver gown for this New Year's bash. Nathan's office had sponsored this lovely fete, which had been planned by Jonas Travel and Events, at the Chase Park Plaza. The room was full of maybe 200 revelers. We were having such a wonderful time. Steak (their signature tenderloin) and lobster for dinner, with loads of champagne. I might have mentioned that.

"You look lovely this evening, Roni," Nathan whispered in my ear. "I'm so glad we booked a room. Maybe after a little more partying, we can head downstairs?" he added with eagerness in his voice.

"How about we take a walk on the terrace," I whispered back. "I know it's cold outside, but it's such a lovely view of the park."

"Of course, that's a nice idea," Nathan said. "Here, let me give you my jacket. You're a little naked in that dress, not that I'm complaining."

We stepped outside into cool, crisp air. The Zodiac Room at the Chase Park Plaza was eleven floors above Forest Park, with a breathtaking view. It was stunning, even in the dark of January. The night was cold but clear, and the stars were out.

"It's lovely out here, isn't it?" I asked Nathan, leaning against his chest.

"Yes, it is a lovely view. I wasn't sure about moving to St. Louis when you first proposed it, but I think it's worked out well," he replied, putting his arms around me.

"I like the sound of 2020. I think this is going to be a stellar year for us, don't you?"

"Yes, I do. We seem to have just about everything," he answered.

"I'd say perfect." I smiled back and kissed him again, this time with more meaning.

"I think it's time to go to our room, don't you?"

"Yes, just one more glass of champagne." I laughed.

We had a lovely evening. My second New Year's resolution was to spend more time with my husband in 2020. We really needed alone time. It would do wonders for our marriage. After a late, long brunch at one of the Chase's excellent restaurants, we headed home. That's when the shine of the New Year started to dim. As we opened the door, we heard trouble from several fronts. Oliver was crying, Katlin was screaming, and Anna was yelling.

"What on earth is going on here?" I demanded.

Anna came from the kitchen with paint all over her and looking like she had been sparring with a bear.

"I tried to do painting with them, but they are just impossible today," she sighed.

"I don't like painting," Oliver screamed. "I want to watch TV." He, too, had paint all over him.

"I want to go to Madelene's skating party, but Anna won't let me. All the girls are going. I can't be the only one not there," she demanded.

"Katlin, you know Anna can't take you somewhere else without permission," I told her. Nathan was trying to calm Oliver down. He was having much more success than I was.

"Well, give me permission NOW," she shouted.

"Don't you shout at me," I shouted back. "If everyone was going to Madelene's party, why didn't I see an invitation?" I asked sharply.

"It's in my school bag, but you never look in there," Katlin snapped.

"Anna, have you seen this invitation?"

"Yes," she answered sheepishly. "I've been away during the holidays and didn't keep up with their school notes. I'm sorry."

"It's not your fault, Anna. Katlin should have said something before we left."

"You were all in a rush and I didn't want to bother you," Katlin replied with hands on her hips. There was something so comical about this little diva I almost wanted to laugh. Almost.

"Do you think this behavior will encourage me to let you go?" I asked. At this, her tears came in a flood.

"You don't know how hard it is at school," she blurted out. "These girls are all in a clique. They go to dance class together and play softball. They wear the same brands and have the same things. I try so hard to be in their group, but I just can't seem to get in. They're so mean to girls who don't have the right stuff. I need this party," she cried.

Now I was at a loss. I had no idea about any of this. Why would sweet, lovely Katlin not be in the cool girls' group?

"OK, Katlin. I'll let you go, but you apologize to Anna. Now."

"Sorr-reee. I have to run and get ready. Find my skates, Anna," the little tyrant demanded as she ran off.

"No problem, Mrs. Wright. I'll get the skates. I know where they are. Do you want me to take her?"

"No, I probably should go and get a look at these bullies," I said, my New Year's bubble now soundly burst.

Anna helped Nathan clean up Oliver as I went to the kitchen. It was a disaster. Paint everywhere. Oliver must have been slinging paint. On the kitchen table, on the island, and—oh no!—on my expensive wallpaper! I would never get all this paint cleaned up. New Year's resolution number three: Stop Oliver from throwing tantrums.

27

I took Katlin to the skating rink and watched as the girls skated. There was definitely a pecking order to these girls. It appeared that Madelene was the leader, or maybe the chief bully. Katlin was trying hard to move up in the pack, but not succeeding. I had absolutely no idea how to deal with bullies or what to tell Katlin. One thing was certain: I didn't like her behavior, and it seemed to be tied to this bully. New Year's resolution number four: Help Katlin navigate the school bully.

January 2 brought a return to sanity. It was a Thursday, so I had drop-off duty. We were all a little sluggish, still recovering from New Year's celebrating, but I think we were all happy to be back to our routine. No matter how crazy life got, returning to our routine seemed to right the world. We arrived at school just in time. The kids slid out of the car and off to their respective classes. Both were less eager to return to school, for entirely different reasons, I suspected. But I was soon back to work. There was a lot to do. No time to ponder my kid's problems. I was leading a group of Boeing executives on a trip to Japan that left January 18.

The year 2020 was looking stellar for Jonas Travel and Events. The Boeing trip to Japan was a pretty short turnaround for such a long trip, but it was all well planned. Before I left for Japan, I had to make sure plans for some of our bigger events were progressing well. We were making all the plans for an Anheuser-Busch InBev convention in Milan at the end of February. It coincided with a major international food and beverage conference. It was Clark's account, and he would be going, but I was going too. I'm better with language issues, and we had two smaller accounts who would be represented there as well.

We also had scheduled a number of entertainment and presentation events that needed careful planning. In early March, we had the Bayer conference in Paris. Bayer was a German company, but they wanted to take their executives to Paris. My German would be helpful there since the company prefers German-speaking managers. Then there was a major banking conference in San Francisco in early April. And that same month would be the World Food Producers conference in New York.

Then, of course, there was the Tokyo Olympics in July. Jonas Travel had contracts for travel promotions with fourteen different groups from all across the globe, all needing translators. I had six other local translators lined up to help. We were working on staggered schedules for the groups so we could handle them all. I'd be mostly supervising, but I was chosen to go because of my language skills. I would probably be in Japan for nearly three weeks. All in all, it was looking like a super busy year. I was going to have trouble with my first two New Year's resolutions. All this travel would no doubt cause more division in my family and not help me get closer to them. My solution? An exotic family vacation. *I'll put Megan on that.*

On Monday, I was back in the gym as usual. I loved my routine. Grace was working me hard.

"You haven't said much about your trip to the Christmas markets. Perhaps you didn't run into anyone interesting there?" she said with a smirk.

"Yes, Grace, I saw Dan," I replied.

"'Saw' with a capital S?" she asked.

"You do like to get all the dirty details, don't you?" I said, flopping on a bench exhausted. "Yes. That's all I'm saying. As it turns out, he's a cad. I'm never seeing him again. Enough said. I had a very good Christmas and New Year's with my family, and I'd like to focus on that."

"Aren't you going to Japan soon?" she asked.

"Yes. The end of next week. I'll miss our workouts all the following week."

"Anyone special with a capital S on the Japan trip?"

"My brother, if that counts," I answered. "He's special, but not what you were looking for, I fear."

"You know I never go anywhere," Grace offered. "That's why I'm so interested in your adventurous life. I have to live vicariously through you."

"I think you prefer the sordid bits." I smiled.

"They are the most interesting. I'm starving for gossip."

"Come on, Grace," I said. "You work in a gym. I expect you hear loads of juicy gossip."

"Oh, but yours has that international flare I like so much," she quipped, reminding me why I liked Grace and coming to this gym so much.

It was just four days now until I left for Japan. Catherine was helping arrange some special entertainment for the Boeing clients in Tokyo. These men were government officials who procured and maintained military aircraft from Boeing. They met every year to review their programs and get to know the people who assist in maintaining the Japanese military aircraft. With threats from North Korea, they were more concerned than ever with having effective aircraft. My job was to make all arrangements for hotels, meals, and entertainment. I would supervise our local staff and provide interpretation whenever needed. Many of the Japanese officials spoke some English, but none of the Boeing people spoke any Japanese. I'd been able to convince them that they needed me to make sure everything is interpreted correctly. It's a pretty good moneymaker for Jonas, and I got to travel to Japan.

I had spent a year in Japan after college teaching English to middle school students. It was a great way to improve my Japanese, and it allowed me to travel across the country. The bonus was meeting Nathan in Japan. Odd that I traveled halfway around the world to meet a boy from Chicago. He was spending a semester studying Japanese architecture. We were both on a weekend tour of sacred shrines. The shrines were beautiful, and Nathan was fascinating. I loved his intelligence and willingness to embrace other cultures. We fell in love with Japan and each other. Six months after I returned from my time in Japan, we were married. I moved to Chicago and started working for Jonas. The rest, as they say, is history. I was always happy for an opportunity to return to Japan.

In my first four years at Jonas, I led tours all over Europe and Japan. It was a good thing I had a minor in history and a love of all things historic. I used this in my tours with a flourish. I took every possible opportunity to learn more history. I seldom forgot any facts. I was hardly home, but when I was, it was like a honeymoon all over again. Absence really did make the heart grow fonder. Nathan had joined me on a couple of trips when I had some R & R time at the end of the tour. He shared my interest in history, especially architectural history. The things he'd taught me on the history of architecture and the things we learned together became part of my tours. After Katlin was born, I had tried to limit my time conducting tours and increase the corporate travel and events. I suppose I still traveled a lot for someone with two children. At least my mother thought so. Nathan didn't say much about it. He knew this was my life when we married, so it's hard for him to complain now. But I sometimes felt that he wasn't comfortable with it. The nanny helps. There's no way I could have done this without a nanny—*we* could have done this, I should say. We've passed through the hardest part now that the kids are in school. Thank God for school. I couldn't imagine where we'd be without it and the nanny.

"Here's your airline tickets," Megan said, coming into my office and waking me from my thoughts.

"Is there anything you need me to do for you while you're gone?" she asked. "Will Nathan need some help?"

"I think we'll be just fine, Megan," I answered, wondering why this interest in Nathan. Maybe she has a crush on him. I was sure that would embarrass him. "If Nathan needs anything, he can always call my mother," I added, hoping to settle the issue.

After she left, I took out a piece of paper and wrote down my New Year's resolutions. I had always been a believer in writing down your goals. This is what I wrote:

**New Year's resolutions for 2020**
1. Spend more time with my kids.
2. Spend more time with my husband.
3. Stop Oliver from throwing tantrums.
4. Help Katlin navigate the bullies at school.
5. Figure out why Megan is so concerned about Nathan.
6. Find a new dimension to my career.

I had to add something career-oriented, and I was feeling like it was time to challenge myself.

The trip to Japan was indeed a challenge. It took nearly 24 hours to fly from St. Louis to Tokyo, with a major stop in Denver. I had hoped that the Boeing executives could commandeer a private plane to fly direct, but that never materialized. Cost cutting, or some such thing. My brother was a salesman of sorts for Boeing, working with its military aircraft division. Japan was one of his accounts, so he was one of the executives making the trip. It made the trip a little easier, but he was more interested in pleasing his superiors than spending time with his big sister. I understood. We were both competitive and career-oriented. I think it's the German blood, or maybe just all the sauerkraut our mother fed us. Either way, the trip was rather tedious, and I was glad to finally be going home.

We left Japan on January 24. I was nearly asleep when my brother dropped into the empty seat next to me.

"Have you heard about this new virus in China? The news just reported that Wuhan, China, is being completely shut down to limit exposure. That has to be pretty serious."

"I'm not familiar with Wu-what?"

"Wuhan," he repeated. "It's a city of eleven million. They say the virus started in an animal market there. It causes pneumonia, and people have even died. The World Health Organization is investigating. It's been found in Thailand and South Korea too. Pretty scary, I'd say."

"Fortunately, we don't have any trips scheduled for those areas this year, so I think I'll be alright."

"Maybe, but if it spreads from person to person, it won't be long before it's everywhere. There's something in this Japanese paper about it. Can you read it?" he asked.

"'The Chinese authorities closed off Wuhan by canceling planes and trains leaving the city and suspending busses, subways and ferries within it,'" I read. "'Seventeen people have died in China and more than 570 have been infected, including one in Japan.' Wow, that was a close call for us, I'd say."

"See, I told you it was scary," Adam said.

"Adam, I don't want to buy trouble before we know more," I told him. "I'm sure the World Health Organization will figure this out and it will all be fine. Can you imagine if places I need to travel were shut down, like Wuhan? It will never reach the U.S., and if it does, they'll find a medical solution and rub it out. There will never be lockdowns in our country. We all rely on travel too much. How would people conduct business or even get to work? No, it just can't happen."

"I think it could be a disaster. Boeing is still trying to recover from the 737 Max disaster," he added in a whisper, as if we weren't all too familiar with the terrible crashes abroad that had grounded the entire fleet of 737s. It had nearly brought Boeing to its knees. "We don't need another problem."

"You worry too much, brother," I said. "We'll be fine…if I can get a little sleep before we get to Denver."

"Good night, Sis. Sleep well, if you can."

We landed rather roughly in Denver in a snowstorm. Every flight east and west was canceled. This was not the way my 2020 was supposed to begin. It was a symmetrical year. Everything should run like clockwork. I didn't have time to spend a night in Denver. The Boeing executives invited me to follow them to a nearby hotel and offered to pay for the night. I didn't have many options, so I took them up on their kind offer. Once in my room, I set myself up to make multiple calls: to the office, to clients, to home. I opened my laptop to work. There was much to do for the AB InBev Convention in Milan. I first called Megan to check on what was happening in the office.

"We're all working as hard as we can," she said. "I think I put in sixty hours last week, covering for you and making travel plans for Milan. I'm pretty sure Catherine has done the same. I know it's only January, but we're all a little stressed. So many events coming up."

"Yes, I know. I call that success," I said a bit tersely. "Why don't you plan an after-work party for next week? Drinks and dinner. Jonas will pay. Make it some place fun, not formal. We can relax and talk. I know we're busy, but that's the reward for success. Maybe I can push for pay increases this year," I offered. "Now, let me talk with Catherine."

I talked with most of the employees. They all had piles of work, but none seemed as stressed or whiny as Megan. I supposed that was her nature, although she had worked with me for four years and I had never noticed it before. Maybe familiarity does breed contempt. I had dinner delivered to my room so I could work. I had networked enough with Boeing. They were my most solid client, but enough was enough.

The snowstorm was pretty intense and widespread. I didn't get home until Sunday afternoon. When I opened the door, Oliver was racing through the house with Anna close on his heels. Katlin was texting school friends on her tablet. Nathan was cleaning a terrible mess in the kitchen.

"Wow, what happened here?" I asked innocently.

"I think my wife has abandoned me, and my kids are out of control," Nathan answered.

"I'm sorry. It was no fun being stuck at the Denver Airport for a day and a half," I answered, a little more sharply than I'd intended. Nathan wasn't usually this angry about my trips. I can't imagine what had changed.

Then I saw what he was doing. There was spaghetti on the walls, floors, and maybe ceiling. Nathan looked up. "Oliver didn't like his lunch," he said.

"Oh," was all I could think of to say. I wanted to ask what his consequences were, but I seemed to be treading on thin ice and I was very tired. "What can I do?"

"Finish this up. I'm going out," he told me as he picked up his coat and left.

"I really need to get back to my dorm," Anna told me with coat in hand. "I wasn't supposed to work this weekend, but Nathan needed help. I have to study," she added then was out the door too.

"Katlin, Oliver," I called, knowing neither would come running. I ordered a pizza, got them bathed, and we all went to bed. Before she retired, Katlin came in my room with her tablet. "Some of the girls have backpacks like this," she said, pointing to a picture on Instagram. "If I don't have one, they won't talk to me."

"Katlin, that backpack is $450. We can't afford that."

"Well, you're working all the time," she said. "Aren't you the boss? That's what I tell my friends anyway."

I drew in a deep breath. "I am the boss, Katlin, but that's a lot of money for a school backpack. If these girls are so mean, why do you want to be their friends?"

"It's just the way it is. You don't understand. Any girl who isn't in the best group has no friends at all. They're all losers. I don't want to be a loser." With this, she stormed off. I had been so wrong about Katlin. I thought she breezed through school. Clearly this was not the case. I had no experience with this sort of thing. I was way out of my element with no idea of how to help my daughter.

Nathan came in just as I was climbing into bed.

"I don't know how I'm going to survive all your trips this year. Maybe we need a full-time nanny. Someone older, perhaps. Someone who can control your kids."

I didn't want to respond to that. Nothing I would say would make it better. He didn't even know the worst of Katlin's problems. The only one who could control Oliver at all was my mother. This was going to be a much longer conversation than I wanted to have after a long day. I was already tired of 2020.

# February 2020 – Too Many Flowers, Not Enough Heart

The third day of February fell on a Monday, so I was in the gym as usual. I only came twice last week, and Grace was working me really hard. I couldn't quite see how this would make up for skipping last Monday, but I humored her until I collapsed on a bench.

"Are you trying to kill me, Grace?" I asked. "I know I missed last Monday, but please don't punish me."

"Sorry, maybe I got carried away. You were awfully whiny last week. Exercise fixes that," she said, smiling.

"Or kills you," I said with a smile. "It's probably good because I'm going out for drinks with the office tonight."

"Any special event?" she asked.

"No, they've just been working really hard, and I thought it would be nice to have a little fun. I do like them all. They're my family."

"I thought you had a husband and two children," she quipped.

"I haven't forgotten. That's why I've waited a week since I got back from Japan. My family didn't handle my last absence very well. Neither family," I told her.

"And drinks will help?"

"Probably not, but I have to try. At least with the work family. I think there might be some dynamic going on I haven't figured out."

"Like romantic entanglements, you mean?" she asked. "Who?"

"I don't know, but there seems to be some tension I can't put my finger on. Maybe I'll learn something tonight."

"I thought you knew all about romantic entanglements," she said, smirking.

"Watch it," I warned. "Remind me why I like you," I said, laughing.

Megan had picked a fun Mexican restaurant for our drinks party. It was perfect because they had a wonderful and filling appetizer list that would serve as dinner and sponge for our alcohol. Everyone seemed in a festive mood. This was not fun for me. It was an opportunity for me to take a measure of what was going on in my office.

I had a side chat with the waitress when I came in and explained I had an "allergy" to alcohol but didn't want to spoil the party, so all my drinks should be tonic with lime—lots of lime. This was my standard "safe" drink. I used it often with clients or whenever I needed a clear head as the drinks flowed. It works like a charm. Everyone thinks I'm drinking too. As they get tipsy, they don't notice I'm not. I sat at the end of the table in full view of everyone and paid attention to everything being said. Much of the early talk centered around our workload. I listened carefully, making mental notes about changes or adjustments I needed to make.

"Did you see that President Trump suspended entry into the United States by any foreign nationals who traveled to China? It's because of the virus thing in China. Wash U has a big student exchange program with China, and we handle a lot of their travel. It would hurt to lose that," Andrew said.

*Note to self: Help Andrew find some new clients.*

"I don't really think that virus is much of a problem for my accounts. Enterprise is so strong. People will always need cars," Kari said confidently.

*Maybe I should see how strong Kari's accounts really are. Overconfidence isn't good either.*

"I'm worried about IT problems at the Olympics. So many things could go wrong there, even hacking. It's so far away. If we can't communicate easily, it could be a disaster," Gavin said.

*Why don't they say these things in our staff meeting? Are they too afraid to raise issues with me? We need a backup communication plan for the Olympics.*

"I just hope we can get through the big events before the Olympics," Catherine said. "I've got three major events to plan and host. I barely get home to see my family these days."

*We need backup staff for Catherine. I'll let her make the selection. Maybe I need a real drink.*

Once we (they) all had had a few drinks, I started picking up on more personal stuff. The first thing I noticed was that Kari and Clark were way chummier than I ever saw in the office. As the night progressed, I saw some definite signs of familiarity, to put it politely.

*Find out if Kari and Clark are having an affair. This can't end well. They're both married.*

"I can't work very late. Somebody has to take care of the kids. My husband is never home and that's just fine with me," Kari spit out with too much anger.

*Have a talk with Kari and find out what's going on with her marriage. Maybe she needs some counseling. If she's involved with Clark, they're in for trouble.*

"I don't have a family to come home to," said Megan, "but if I did, I wouldn't see enough of them."

"I think you already see enough of *him*," Sarah said, giggling.

Megan jabbed her roughly in the ribs and said softly, "Shut up."

*Find out if Megan is having an affair. She's not married, so it must be some sort of illicit entanglement or she wouldn't shush Sarah so roughly. That can't end well either.*

I had ordered a limousine to take everyone home but me, since I wasn't really drinking. As soon as I got home, I took out my notebook and wrote down all the notes I had stored in my head. It was a little overwhelming. I didn't expect to find out so much, particularly all the relationship problems. Made me think about my own relationship. Were we on shaky ground too?

"Nathan, I'd like to take the family on a nice trip over spring break. What do you think?" I asked next morning over breakfast. It wasn't often that we had breakfast together, but I wanted to make sure we did today.

"When is spring break?" he asked. I'd been hoping for a simple yes.

"Let's see," I replied, pulling up my phone. "It's the week of March 23. I was thinking we could go to New York. Maybe take Anna to watch the kids at night while we see a show or two. Romantic dinner, maybe?" I added, trying to be flirtatious.

"I don't know. I have that design for the University of Nebraska due by the end of March. I'm afraid I'll be too busy. Can you go without me? Oh, by the way, I have to go to Nebraska next week for some preliminary planning," he added.

My heart sank. It wasn't like Nathan to nix a romantic anything. I'd been so hopeful for spring break. Somehow, I thought one nice trip would solve everything. After all, that is what I sell. "OK," I said. "I guess it can't be helped. Maybe I'll plan a trip to Disney World with the kids. If you can make it, great. If not, we'll get along."

"That's my girl," Nathan said, giving me a quick kiss. "You're the expert at planning trips. Don't forget, you're taking the kids to school today," he said as he flew out the door.

I decided on the plan. We'd leave Saturday, March 21, as soon as spring break began, and come back the following Saturday. I'd have Sarah make plans for me. Megan clearly had too much on her plate, and I needed Sarah to have more practice at this type of thing. I gave her basic directions and would see what accommodations she came up with.

The second thing I did that morning was call Catherine in and talk to her about hiring an assistant. She was delighted. Next, I spoke with Gavin about alternate IT plans for the Olympics. He suggested he coordinate plans with the New York office. I think he thought I was a genius. I had to agree.

The next day I sat with Megan to arrange redistributing some of her work. She didn't take it very well. I think she thought I was demoting her.

"I want you to know I hear you," I explained. "I know you're overworked, and I want to find a way to take some of the stress off you."

I must have said the wrong thing because she looked at me and ran from the room. Maybe I'm not as good a leader as I thought. Clearly I was missing something.

Valentine's Day was strange. I got two lovely bouquets. One, of course, from Nathan, but a much bigger one from Dan. I was perplexed. I had only spoken to Dan a couple of times since our time in Munich. I actually hadn't thought of him at all. But his bouquet was massive. It was pretty embarrassing. I immediately threw out the card and told the office it was from Boeing as a thank you for the Japanese trip. Still, I was getting sideways glances. But not nearly as many as Kari, who also got two bouquets. One card made her blush. Had I seen a questioning look at Clark? The other bouquet contained just one dark-colored rose. And poor Catherine got a very small bouquet from her husband. It sent her to the bathroom crying. Too many flowers, not enough heart.

Right after Valentine's Day came Oliver's sixth birthday. Megan had made all the arrangements for me. I just had to show up with a gift. We had invited his whole class to a private session at the Magic House, as well as my parents and my sister Korie and her family. Adam came too. It was a great party with very little for me to do. They provided decorate-your-own-cupcakes for dessert and lots of activities. After the main party, the kids were free to roam through the museum until they dropped with exhaustion. Of course, Oliver never dropped, but Anna, who was chasing him, did. We went home for pizza and the cake my mother had brought. It was a nice time, and Oliver was happy.

But that happiness was short-lived. The dark cloud that appeared on Valentine's Day was just the tip of the iceberg. As reports of the new virus started dominating the news, we were all on edge. Then the bomb dropped on February 23. Europe was facing a major outbreak, especially in Italy. As the number of cases grew from fewer than five to more than 150 southeast of Milan, government officials locked down towns. They closed schools and canceled sporting events and all cultural events, including the AB InBev convention. I estimated that we had put about 300 hours into planning that convention. I just couldn't believe it could get canceled over a simple virus. Clark delivered the devastating news. One by one, all our accounts scheduled for this exposition canceled. Things were getting even worse.

"AB InBev just told me they're canceling all foreign travel," Clark told me. "It doesn't make sense."

"Isn't this just a China thing?" I asked. "I thought most people who got it had traveled to China."

"The CDC has confirmed someone in California has the virus but has never traveled or been in contact with someone who traveled to China. They're saying this is something called 'community spread,'" Clark read from his phone.

"But still, there are only, what, fifteen cases in the U.S.?" I argued. "Why all the panic?"

"Washington University says this type of virus can cause a pandemic. Thousands of people could die," Andrew told us, entering the room. "I'm afraid Wash U is going to postpone or cancel all the foreign study programs. That's a huge part of my accounts."

"I know this looks bad," I said, "but surely it won't last long. The flu season comes and goes. We have the smartest medical minds in the world—many right here in St. Louis. We'll ride this out. Besides, all these companies we represent still have to have meetings and conventions. If foreign travel is out, then we can at least book some meetings here. There aren't any cases in St. Louis yet. Maybe some of these companies would like to come here for their meetings?"

I don't know how reassuring I managed to be, but at least I gave them something to work on.

Then the second shoe dropped. Bayer called and said the conference in Paris was canceled. My world was unraveling.

I hadn't been paying any attention to the virus. By the end of February, there were only 18 confirmed cases in the U.S. and five deaths. I couldn't understand the panic.

# March 2020 – Life Locked Down

Just as we were finding some success in setting up corporate meetings in cities with no reported virus cases, the Centers for Disease Control and Prevention (CDC) put a stop to our last hope. The CDC posted a recommendation that all gatherings be limited to fifty people. No companies were going to pay for us to organize a meeting of less than fifty people. Every client that was making plans for a domestic conference canceled. We were left with almost nothing to do.

"I know this all looks really bad," I announced at our Monday morning meeting on March 9. "But this virus thing can't last forever. Perhaps we should put our efforts into rescheduling events. Do any of you have clients who might want to reschedule travel or conferences?" I asked.

"Reschedule for when?" Kari replied. "Do you know when this will all be over?"

"Viruses are a winter thing, right?" I offered with more hope than I felt. "Surely by midsummer the country should be traveling again, at least domestically. See if you can work on rescheduling things."

"And if no one is rescheduling?" Clark asked. "Then what?"

"Well, I'm taking my kids to Disney World," I said gleefully. "Don't look at me like that. I know things look grim, but you've all been complaining about having too much work to do. So now is a good time to take a break. I think half of the office could schedule a vacation now and no one would notice."

"I'd like to take off for spring break," Kari replied. "My family would be thrilled."

"OK, Kari is going to be off the week of March 23 with me. Who else?"

I had a few more nervous takers. But life was no longer a perfect well-oiled machine. Everything was falling apart.

The one constant I still had was the gym. "I don't know what I'd do without you to keep me moving," I said to Grace, panting hard as she once again was pushing me to my limit.

"Don't worry," Grace replied. "I'm not going anywhere until you can run a marathon."

"Or have a heart attack and drop dead," I joked.

"Just for that, ten more minutes on the bike," she demanded. I was so glad I still had Grace to ground me or, rather, to keep me moving.

But it didn't take long for everything else to fall apart.

St. Louis County announced their first confirmed virus patient on March 13. Two days later, Disney World announced it was closing all its parks. My world was crumbling around me. I was still determined to have some fun with my family.

"I'm so sorry we can't go to Disney World," I told my family that night. "But we can still have fun right here in St. Louis. What would you like to do?"

"I want to go the Science Center," said Katlin. "There are so many interesting things there."

"I want to go to the Magic House," said Oliver. "I love that place. Maybe the zoo too."

"I'd like to take a walk through the Botanical Gardens," I told them.

"They have a great kids' play area," Katlin reminded me. "We had so much fun there the last time we went."

"OK. I'll make a schedule." I smiled, feeling much better. We weren't going to let this thing lock us up at home.

I couldn't have been more wrong.

My brother came to visit that night. "The Boeing offices are closing," he said. "I'll be working from home, but I'm worried about my job. Ever since the 737 disaster, Boeing has been in trouble. Now with flights grounded everywhere, no new planes will be ordered. I think layoffs are coming soon," he told me. "On top of that, Melissa and I broke up."

"Oh, Adam, I'm so sorry. Is there any chance you might get back together?"

"With Boeing or Melissa?" he asked, smiling wryly.

"You're not losing your job at Boeing," I told him.

"I don't think I'm enough for Melissa, whatever that means."

"I thought she was the one, Adam."

"Yeah, I did too," he said. "This means there won't be any work for you from Boeing."

"There doesn't seem to be any work for Jonas anywhere right now," I said.

"What will you do?" he asked.

"Well, Nathan is working from home now. I'm still manager of Jonas Travel, we just don't have any work. I can't imagine that Jonas will last without people traveling. No matter how I try to spin it, I can't see a future right now. Travel is all I've ever known." The truth of what I was saying suddenly struck me like a brick, and tears started falling fast.

The following week, the St. Louis County Executive announced new restrictions. A stay-at-home order would go into effect March 23. Everything was shutting down. My office and Nathan's office would have to close. I wondered if school would reopen after spring break.

Instead of a vacation or staycation, I went to the office to deliver the bad news. I called the whole staff into a meeting. "Since we are not essential workers, our office will have to close," I told them. "We can still work from home, so take everything you need to continue working."

"How long will this last?" Megan asked.

"I have no idea," I told them. "I haven't heard much from our corporate office. They're shutting down too, as are most of our clients.

Most are working from home, but I can't imagine they will have any work for us."

"What about the Olympics?" Clark asked. "Are you still working on that?"

"As of this minute, yes, but there is talk of canceling the Olympics."

"That's the last thing on our schedule!" Megan nearly shouted.

"I know. I don't know what else to say. Take your stuff home. I'll call if I hear any news."

Nearly everyone had tears in their eyes. I wished I had something more to tell them. I wished I could find some rainbow. But it was all clouds. No sun. No rainbow. We all left early with hugs. Kari and Clark weren't even trying to hide their feelings. Clearly this was going to be hard for us all.

I came home with two computers and piles of paper from my office. I set them down in our huge foyer and saw Anna standing there with all her luggage packed.

"Are you taking a spring break too?" I asked.

She didn't lift her head or look at me. He voice was so low I could barely hear it. "I'm going back to Germany. I booked a flight tonight. So many borders are closing, I don't want to be stuck here, away from my family," she murmured.

"Anna, no, you don't have to leave," I begged. "We'll take care of you. You are our family."

"You know that's not true." She lifted her head and looked at me, tears now streaming down her face. "I'm really just a servant. You need me, but I'm not family. I can't control Oliver, and I don't know how to help Katlin. They need their mother, not a nanny. I need my family. I'm sorry."

"No, I'm sorry. If you feel like this, then it's my fault. I should have treated you better," I said with tears in my eyes too.

"It doesn't matter. I need to go home. It's time," she told me.

"What about your studies at Wash U? Will you finish your degree?" I asked.

"My degree is very important, but I can take classes online. I've talked with mine professors. At some point, I can transfer to a college in Germany. This is not an easy decision, but I think it's the right one for me. I do want to thank you for bringing me here. It's been very good for me, but it's time to go. Here is my address. You can send my last paycheck here. I have said goodbye to the children. I think I should leave now." She was looking and feeling much more confident than I had ever seen her.

We hugged and she left. *What now? How do I find a way to work at home with no nanny?* I'd never been without a nanny. I slid down the wall, tears coming fast.

Just then the door opened, and Nathan came in with his own home office equipment and boxes of papers. He set them down and came over to me.

"What's wrong?" he asked, full of concern. "Has something happened?"

"Our life is just unraveling," I answered, tears streaming down my face.

Bounding down the stairs, Katlin cried, "Anna's gone. Mommy's crying because Anna left. I'm sad too. Oliver is just being mean."

"Is this true?" Nathan asked.

"Yes," I managed to get out through my tears. "Anna's gone back to Germany. My office is closed. I have to work from home, but I don't have any work to do. Most of the meetings and events have been canceled for the next two months. I don't know what I'll do."

Nathan sat on the floor next to me, and Katlin came and put her arms around me. It had been a very long time since we'd hugged like this. Oliver ran into our family hug with more force than I thought he possessed.

"Are we playing a game?" he asked. "I want to play."

"No, Oliver," Nathan told him. "Mommy and Katlin are sad that Anna left."

"Oh, that," he said. "She was kind of mean."

"No, she wasn't," Katlin argued. "You were horrible to her."

"Enough," I said. "Things are going to be different now. Mommy and Daddy can't go to their offices because of this virus. We have to all stay in our house for a while."

"Yay, it's a party!" Oliver screamed.

"No, Oliver, it's terrible," Katlin countered. "We can't go to Disney World. We can't go to the Science Center or the zoo or the Magic House. We can't go anywhere because of this stupid virus. It's awful."

"I know it's bad, but we are going to find a way to make the best of it," I told them with much more optimism than I felt.

"Can we go anywhere for spring break?" Katlin asked.

"We could take walks," I told them. "We're lucky we live in a city with many lovely parks."

"Can we go to Grandma Krieger's?" Katlin asked. "That's always fun."

"Maybe," I answered. "I'll have to ask, but that's a good idea, Katlin."

"One thing we must do now," Nathan interjected, "is get dinner."

"One thing we can do is order out food. How about we order a great big bowl of spaghetti from the Pasta Hut?" I asked. The answer to that question was always the same: a resounding yes. Even though we couldn't go to restaurants, we could order out. Many offered contactless pickup. You paid online and gave a description of your vehicle, then someone ran out with your food and put it in your car. No contact. No danger.

The next day, we figured out how to set up offices in our house. Nathan ran to Office Max and bought a desk that he put up in the living room. It seemed like a nice cozy space to work. I was going to use my little office off the kitchen where I managed household papers. Now it would be my work office too. It was small and cramped, but I managed to set up a computer and put papers in order.

Next, I called my mother and asked if we could come for a couple of days. She was, of course, delighted to have us. Nathan still had to work, so it would be just me and the kids. That seemed like a perfect break to us.

On Monday morning, we drove to Washington, a sleepy little town on the banks of the Missouri River steeped in history. My parents had a house with a couple of acres on the north side of town. It was only a mile from the river. My mother had taught fifth grade at the local school for 25 years but was now retired. My father was a family doctor but kept some hours at Mercy Hospital of Washington. They welcomed us with loving, open arms. The kids ran to them, and big hugs were shared all around. Mom made a lovely lunch of grilled cheese and tomato soup—homemade, of course. The kids were delighted to feed the chickens and run around the property with my parents' dog Daisy. She was a mutt but as loveable as a dog could be. For dinner, we had Mom's famous fried chicken with all the trimmings. It felt so good to be someplace that felt safe.

The next morning, I woke to the smell of coffee brewing and cinnamon rolls baking. I quickly dressed and joined my parents downstairs. I poured a cup of coffee and grabbed their copy of the *St. Louis Post-Dispatch*. The headline read: "Tokyo Olympics Postponed." I let out a sigh closer to a scream.

"What's the matter, dear?" Mom asked.

"The Olympics," I stammered. "It was my last big booked event for 2020. Now it's gone. I can't imagine what will happen to my business. I'm afraid we'll be ruined."

"Surely it can't be as bad as all that? We've only had a few cases here in Missouri. Maybe it won't even come here."

"Make no mistake," I told her firmly, "it will come here. The U.S. is on the brink of becoming the center for the virus. The reports out of

New York City are terrifying. Some of my colleagues there are leaving the city and moving in with any relatives that will take them. My business is based on two things: business travel and conventions. The virus has basically shut down those things completely. I don't know what I'm going to do."

"Nathan's job is secure, isn't it?" she asked, coming over to sit with me.

"Yes, Nathan is working harder than ever," I answered. "We're not going to starve, although, if my business fails, the house may be more than we can handle on one salary."

"You always have us," my father said, smiling. "We'll be here whenever you need us. The virus won't come to Washington. It seems strongest in the cities where people are packed in together."

"That's why we're here," I told him. "In St. Louis County, everything is closed. People are ordered—no, asked—to stay home except for grocery stores or other critical needs. With two kids on spring break, I couldn't survive like that. We had first planned a trip to Disney World for spring break, then a staycation in St. Louis."

"So, we're your third choice?" my mother asked.

"No, you were always the best choice," I said, with a little smile that I hoped hid the truth she had guessed.

"Best choice in a pandemic," my father said, laughing.

It did prove to be the best choice. Mom made a lovely picnic with leftover fried chicken, and we ate at a park overlooking the wide Missouri River. It was a fun park with a lot of things for the kids to do. We all came home exhausted. The kids were happy to get a little screen time.

"Since I'm going to be home a lot, maybe I should do more cooking," I told my mother. "Could you teach me some cooking tips?"

"I'd be delighted. Come cook with me," she offered. We made spaghetti to rival the Pasta Hut, and my kids gobbled it up. Mom taught me to add a little nutrition by putting diced carrots in the sauce. Even picky Katlin didn't notice. The next two days, we had all sorts of adventures. The kids had mostly outdoor adventures, while I had some cooking adventures. All too soon it was time for us to go home. But before we did, I had one more surprise.

"I just got an email from the kids' school that says they won't be going back to the classroom because of the virus," I told the family.

"Yay, no school!" Oliver said.

"How will we learn?" shouted Katlin.

"Oh… I'll miss my friends," Oliver realized.

"I don't have the answers to any of that. I don't know what's going to happen." I sighed.

"I have an idea," my mother told me. "Just give me some time."

We all sat feeling very gloomy for most of an hour. Finally, my mother came in with a box of assorted papers.

"I found some old lesson materials you could use to work with," she told me.

The first one I picked up was a Bible lesson. "I thought you taught in a public school?"

"Yes, but I also taught Sunday School for nearly thirty years. I still teach sometimes. Some of these lessons are Sunday School lessons. I thought they'd be closer to Katlin's and Oliver's skill levels. It would be something different."

Sunday School had always been a big area of disagreement between me and my mom. I knew she was a devoted Sunday School teacher, but I've never been good at taking my kids. Seems kind of late to start. I don't know how good I'd be at teaching them.

"There are some fun activities in this box," she offered. "They involve reading and writing. That should keep some of their learning going. And," she added, pulling out another box, "here are puzzles and games that will help as well."

I sat hard on the floor. "How am I going to help with this? I do still have a job, you know."

"But I thought you said there wasn't much to do?" Mom replied. "I know you will figure it out."

I was not at all so sure. I didn't even spend that much time with my kids. Now I was supposed to be home with them every single day! I wasn't a teacher. No way, no how. I felt as low as I had ever felt. I think my mother saw the fear in my face.

"Let's all gather around," she ordered. "We're going to say a little prayer." We sat in a circle on the floor as she directed, holding hands, and she prayed, "Dear Father God, please guide this family through this very difficult time. Help them find a path through their difficulties and challenges. Keep us all safe from the terrible virus and help restore our lives. In Jesus' name we pray." Then we all said, "Amen."

The drive home was somber. Even Oliver, for once, was quiet.

Monday morning came with no routine and no order. Only Nathan got up and started work at his desk in the living room. Oliver got up around seven and watched TV. Katlin and I got up around eight. I went to the kitchen and poured some breakfast cereal. Oliver was screaming for something, but I had no idea what. Nathan was screaming that Oliver had to stop screaming. Katlin was screaming for them to stop screaming. I was lost. I had no energy to scream. I had no gym to go to. It, too, was closed down. I had no office to run. I had kids to…do what with? I was good in the gym. I was very good at my job. I had no idea how to do this, whatever this was. My mother had said a prayer, so I tried that. I sat silently and asked God to give me strength to stop the screaming. Then it came to me.

"Ahhhhhh!" I screamed so loudly that when I finished, the room was quiet.

"What was that?" Nathan asked.

"I thought this was a screaming contest," I said.

"I don't like your screaming," Katlin and Oliver said, nearly in unison. Wow, they agreed on something.

"Screaming doesn't solve anything, does it?" I asked. They all shook their heads. "So, here's the deal, if you scream, I'll scream." I was met with three blank stares.

"OK, Oliver, why were you screaming?" I asked.

"I want something to eat."

"OK, Nathan, why were you screaming?" I asked.

"I was on an important call and Oliver was screaming."

"And Katlin?"

"My ears were hurting from all the screaming."

"Alright, we'll start with Oliver. What do you want to eat?"

"I want Cheerios."

"Cheerios it is, but we must all be very quiet so Daddy can work. OK?" Three heads nodded in agreement. *Wow, my first crisis solved. I'm a genius.*

That's pretty much how the rest of the day went. I dug into Mom's box of lessons and found some things for Oliver and Katlin to do. That lasted a little while. Then Oliver got restless and ran into the living room, disturbing Nathan's work. Nathan got angry, and I took the kids for a walk. I made my mother's spaghetti for dinner while Katlin and Oliver watched TV—which would have been OK if they didn't spend most of the time fighting, which brought Nathan out of his "office" again.

"I have to go to the store," I told Nathan. "You're in charge until I get back."

The grocery store seemed like an oasis compared to the battles at home. I found all the fruit and vegetables on my list and headed to the dry goods aisle. When I got there, I stopped dead in my tracks. The shelves were totally bare. No toilet paper. No paper towels. No hand soap. No cleaning products. No bleach. I found a store employee.

"Where is everything?" I demanded, panic rising in my chest.

"I'm sorry, ma'am," he answered, "people are cleaning off the shelves as soon we fill them up. We put everythin' out as soon as the truck arrives."

"That's just crazy," I said. "What am I supposed to use for toilet paper?"

"I don't know what to say," he said. "You might try the drugstore or Sam's."

I went from store to store and found empty shelves everywhere. This was insane. Almost apocalyptic. At Sam's, as I entered the store, I saw a big sign that read, "Quantities of toilet paper, hand sanitizer, and cleaning supplies are limited. One to a customer. No exceptions."

What a crazy world. An attendant handed out one pack of toilet paper to each customer. With two small kids, nothing is more important than toilet paper. At least this would last us a few weeks. Shopping had become a war zone.

When the kids were finally in bed that night, Nathan and I had some time to talk over a bottle of wine.

"This isn't working," I began, draining my first glass of wine.

"No shit," Nathan exclaimed, draining his glass too. "How long will school be out?"

"I have absolutely no idea. So far, they've only sent the one message saying school is closed for now. Surely it can't be closed for long. The kids have to go to school. We *have* to send our kids to school. I'm not a teacher."

"I have to work," Nathan added. "How can I work with the kids running around the house?"

"Hopefully this won't be for long. Surely something will happen. Maybe the school district will figure out how to open school safely. Maybe your office will reopen. Maybe the virus will disappear," I said, not believing any of it. "Maybe we need more wine." At least that we could both agree on. Wine and vodka and gin and maybe some bourbon too.

On March 31, the St. Louis County Health Department issued a notification of the third virus-related death. In New York, the virus was spreading so fast the CDC issued a request for residents of New York, New Jersey, and Connecticut to avoid travel for fourteen days. Nothing changed. Nothing got better. The only good thing that happened was March was over.

By the end of March, there were about 4,300 deaths in the U.S. and almost 197,000 confirmed cases of the virus. The tide was rising.

# April 2020 –
# When It Rains, It Pours

On April 1, I picked up my calendar, as I did at the beginning of every month—usually to see what we had coming up and what I needed to add—and started crossing off everything. I had already crossed off the March trip to Paris. Now I crossed off this month's planned trip to the banking conference in San Francisco. I slashed through the conference in New York. And with a little more pain, I crossed off the two Broadway shows to which I had tickets. An old college girlfriend was going to go with me to one and Dan the other. Broadway, closed. New York, closed. All crossed off, as was the St. Louis Symphony concert to which we had tickets. Canceled. Hockey, canceled. Three birthday parties, canceled. My appointment at the nail salon, canceled. Hairdresser, canceled. Canceled, canceled, canceled. April was looking so gloomy.

The only exercise I was getting was walking through one of our beautiful parks with the kids. Sometimes, we took bikes and rode a trail. But with April came gloom and rain and even that little bit of escape became impossible. Then the St. Louis County Executive closed all county parks. We were now required to wear a mask if we were out in public, especially indoors, and to stay six feet apart wherever we were. The gloom was growing daily. My life had no order. We were in free fall.

On April 9, we got a big shot in the arm, as it were, when $2,400 appeared in our checking account—a gift from the U.S. government. Officially the money was part of the Economic Impact Payment, but people usually just called them stimulus checks. We just called it salvation. Like many families, we weren't sure how we would make ends meet. This money was a gift from heaven—or the government, depending on your point of view.

By the second week of April, our school district was making an effort at learning. They asked parents to pick up "home learning packets" from the school. When I drove up to the school, someone handed me the packet for our kids' grade levels. But when I got home, there was little explanation about the work. It was terribly disorganized and made little sense to me. Katlin wanted to learn more, and Oliver wanted to learn less. I just wanted more alcohol. Lots more. I decided hard times called for hard alcohol. Wine could get me through lunch, but by dinner time, I needed a cocktail.

I set up a place in the basement family room for the kids to study. I tried hard to make Oliver work on letters and sight words. He would work with me for maybe thirty minutes, then he'd start disrupting everything I did. He'd rip papers and run away. Meanwhile, Katlin was trying to figure out her lessons with great frustration. She didn't know what was wanted of her, and I couldn't figure it out either. Oliver did everything in his considerable ability to disrupt our efforts. Most sessions ended with all three of us crying.

Not only was I failing at trying to teach my kids, I was failing at keeping them out of Nathan's living room office. Every time Oliver ran away from me, he ran right into one of Nathan's meetings. No order. No peace. No joy.

I was also trying to find out where Jonas Travel was going—yes, pun intended. I was communicating with most of our staff, asking them to make calls to clients and potential clients. We hoped to at least reschedule events and trips to late summer or fall. Of course, we had no idea when things might get better, but at least it was something to do. I thought we should stay in touch with clients. I talked to my boss in New York a couple of times a week. He had little to say. Mostly he thought we would have to "ride it out." But I knew there was no money coming in, and we had staff all over the country. I worried about it constantly.

Dan called and wanted to try to get together. I was surprised that he was so dense. Surely someone as smart and together as Dan could see that couldn't happen during a pandemic in any scenario. I was beginning to doubt how smart or together he was. After what I saw in Germany, I suspect he had bigger problems than I could or would help with. He was probably having considerable trouble being home with his family. I felt sorry for him, but I had my own problems to deal with. Besides, Dan was a reminder of something I was trying hard to forget, something I knew could destroy our fragile family. I just hoped he and his problems stayed in Chicago, far away from me, while I tackled my own issues in St. Louis.

We finally made it to the weekend, which was Easter weekend. With all our normal Easter activities canceled, I had to find a way to enjoy some measure of Easter. Churches in our area were still closed, so that was out. The community center where we always went to hunt eggs and visit the Easter bunny was closed. The mall was closed. But I was determined. I saw an ad for Target that said I could buy online and pick up my purchases in the store. That would work perfectly. It came with the bonus of less time shopping in the store and minimal contact with other people, which meant minimal exposure. I picked out a new Easter outfit for each of the kids, Easter baskets filled with goodies, cute stuffed bunnies, candy-filled eggs, egg-decorating kits, and a few other surprises.

Sam's also offered curbside pickup. I bought a ham and rolls and a coconut cake. My parents had agreed to come for a short visit if we stayed outside. Most authorities agreed that we were less likely to get the virus outside. The danger was greater inside and for older adults. So, an outdoor Easter celebration it would be.

Adam was coming too. We decorated our picnic table for Easter brunch. My sister Korie was a nurse at St. Mary's Hospital and thought it was better if they stayed home. My parents planned to drop by Korie's house for an Easter egg hunt when they left our house. Mom had sent me the link to a local church that had a service on YouTube. I wasn't sure I saw the point, but I agreed to attend a virtual church service together. I dyed eggs and wrapped a few fun gifts.

On Easter morning, my parents and Adam came. We sat in our TV room dressed in our Easter best and all watched a church service. It was nice. The kids got restless and started being silly, but who cared? We were, after all, at home. Nathan played Easter Bunny and hid all the goodies while we finished with the Easter service. The rest of the day was outside. The kids had a good time hunting eggs and loved all the goodies. My mother had added kites, yard games, and bubbles to the surprises. The kids and the guys played with the games while my mother and I served brunch on the picnic table. Oliver refused to touch the ham, but he devoured the quiche my mother brought. The coconut cake was delicious. When we had finished brunch, Adam said he had an announcement.

"I'm afraid my job here with Boeing is in jeopardy," he told us. "Boeing hasn't recovered from the 737 debacle, and now with the airlines grounded because of this virus, they are canceling orders. I know there will be layoffs."

"Certainly not you," I started.

"Let me finish, Roni," he interrupted my interruption. "Nobody is truly safe right now. I've been offered a position with corporate in Seattle, and I've decided to take it."

"You're not leaving us?" my mother cried.

"I'm not leaving you, Mother, but I am moving to Seattle. I've already put my house on the market, and I've received multiple contracts. It seems houses are in short supply, just like toilet paper. Since we're all working from home anyway, I will stay here for a month or two before I leave."

Suddenly everything was very still. I felt like I had just been kicked in the stomach. It had been such a beautiful day. We hadn't had a day so enjoyable in ages. Why did he have to spoil it?

"I know my timing stinks," Adam added. "I'm truly sorry for that. I know it will be hard for you, but I thought I should tell you in person, while we're all together. I believe this is the best decision for me. I need to find a new place. St. Louis has nothing more to give me, except all of you and Korie."

I knew this had something to do with the breakup with Melissa. I think he had been ready to walk down the aisle when they broke up. Perhaps he was right. Perhaps a new city would be good for him. There was no doubt that a position in corporate was too good to turn down and probably safer when cuts came. But I didn't want to see him go. Neither did Mom. I could see tears forming in her eyes even as she struggled to hold them back.

"I guess we'll have to plan a trip to Seattle this summer," my mother bravely offered. "I've always wanted to visit Seattle. But please be safe, my dear."

"Seattle is a virus hot spot now, so I'm going to wait until it's a little better there," he told us. "The good thing is, apartment prices there have been plummeting."

The mood had definitely taken a sharp downturn. Both Katlin and Oliver hugged Adam and said they'd miss him, but then they ran off to play with new toys and blow bubbles. After my parents left, Adam and I had a chance to talk while watching the kids play in the backyard.

"I'm so happy for your promotion," I said with much more enthusiasm than I felt. "I know it's a good opportunity for you, but we'll miss you terribly."

"I'll miss you all too. We'll have to FaceTime often," he said, giving me a big hug. "There's something else you need to know, Roni," he added, looking very serious. "It's about Jonas Travel. I'm pretty sure Boeing will be dropping Jonas as a vendor."

"Did I do something wrong? Did I offend somebody?" I jumped in quickly.

He held up a hand. "You don't let a person finish, Roni," he said, smiling. "It has nothing at all to do with you or anybody at Jonas. You've always been a consummate professional. Everybody at Boeing says that. Part of the cost-cutting program is no more traveling. Even if the virus would allow us to travel, no one is going anywhere. It just makes sense from a budget perspective."

"You, my dear brother, already sound like corporate." I smiled half-heartedly.

After he left, the kids were watching TV in a total sugar coma, and I poured myself a large cocktail. Nathan noticed.

"It's a little early for that, isn't it?" he asked.

"Adam said Boeing is dropping Jonas Travel," I told him, taking a big drink. "Do you know what that means? They're our biggest client. I don't know how we'll recover from that."

"Wow, that is big. What will you do?"

"I don't think there is anything I can do," I said. "Nobody is traveling. Nobody is planning corporate meetings or conventions. I don't know how we'll survive."

"You mean how Jonas Travel will survive. We, my dear, our family will be OK," he said with a broad smile. Just then, Oliver smacked Katlin on the top of her head and screamed that he wanted to watch his program. Katlin smacked him back as they both began crying at the top of their lungs.

"Well, maybe," I sighed, sending a smile back to Nathan. For once, Nathan took control of the situation. After all, it was Easter.

I didn't have the courage to call my boss and tell him that Boeing was no longer a client. There was, after all, no official notice. But with all the news, it was unavoidable. I was—or rather, had been—good at what I did. I never made a single misstep with Boeing, and yet, I lost a client. The same was true with all our clients. AB was in better shape, but they had no need for our services. Enterprise was now floundering like many companies that relied on travel, and they weren't even talking to us. Many of the smaller clients weren't answering the phone either.

Kari, Sarah, and Susan were all in the same boat as me. They were trying to teach children at home with little success. Megan was…what was Megan? Very weird, for sure. She showed up at my house twice for no apparent reason. She asked for Nathan once, but he was in a meeting online. She seemed to be unraveling. I understood her worry about the job. She had no second income. But still, there was something very weird going on with her I couldn't quite put my finger on. Gavin was actively looking for another position. I was sure, among all our staff, he would survive the best. There's always somebody looking for an IT person.

Dan called again. I honestly had nothing to say to him. He thought I should find a reason to take a trip up to Chicago. I didn't. Even if there wasn't a once-in-a-century pandemic, I wasn't about to run up to Chicago to see Dan. I had a family. He had a family. I loved my husband. I didn't love Dan. He was a mistake. A terrible, unforgivable, shameful mistake. The more removed I was from Jonas Travel, the more I saw what a sinful blunder Dan had been. I only hoped I could convince him that it was an error for us both. I had enough problems. I didn't need my failure exploding in an already stormy season.

The news was grimmer every day. I knew I should stop watching the news, but it was like taking your eyes from a train wreck. I had to watch. I couldn't wrap my brain around these numbers. When I talked to Korie, she had an even more dire assessment. She said medical workers everywhere were desperate for personal protection equipment. As the number of virus patients soared, masks, gloves, and gowns were all in high demand and short supply. In hot spots, nurses and doctors were reusing these vital supplies. Manufacturers and distribution chains couldn't keep up.

On the last day of April, just as I thought we had made it through the month, my boss called to tell me they were closing the St. Louis office. Actually, they were closing all the offices. Everyone, except for a skeleton staff in New York, would lose their jobs, including me. I should have known it was coming, but it was so hard to hear. I sat on the floor and cried. I mixed myself a stiff drink, called each of my employees, and gave them the terrible news. Then I went to bed. Of course, I was drunk by that time. I just hoped Nathan would put the kids to bed.

Just as I was staggering into bed, Dan called.

"Roni, what are we going to do without our jobs? How will we see each other?"

"I'm drunk, Dan," I told him (at least, I think that's what I said). "I don't want to see you. I'm going to take care of my family, and I think you should do the same. But now I'm going to bed," and I promptly fell asleep.

April was over, and the U.S. had recorded more than 1,000,000 confirmed cases of the virus, nearly a third of all the world's cases. Almost 55,000 people in the U.S. had died. The new terms we learned were shelter-in-place, social distancing, quarantine, and virtual everything. Mask wearing— not just for bandits anymore—was a part of life everywhere.

# May 2020 –
# No Job, No May Flowers

On the first day of May, I once again picked up my calendar and struck through everything that had been canceled. Aunt Mary's and Uncle Stan's fiftieth wedding anniversary, canceled. Nathan's cousin's wedding in Mexico, canceled. Nathan's father's seventieth birthday party, canceled. Baseball, canceled. Dinner with friends, canceled. Canceled, canceled, canceled. It seemed like life itself was canceled.

Without my income, I knew our budget would be stretched thin. I was worried that we wouldn't be able to make all our payments. Although Nathan tried his best to be reassuring, I could tell he was worried too.

"We'll have to make some economies," he announced. "Glenda will have to go. I'm sure you can handle that. The lawn service will have to go too. And I expect you can find other places to cut our budget. I need you to handle this, Roni. I have to go to work." With that, he was off to his office, and I was left with the mess. Glenda had been our cleaning lady for years, but she was the most obvious casualty of the new budget. She took it well.

"I'm actually glad you don't need me anymore," she told me the next day when I gave her the news. "To tell the truth, it makes me nervous to go into people's homes. What if someone had the virus? I'd get it, then my whole family. Better be poor than dead," she added. Good point, I thought. What a choice.

I took a deep breath as I looked at the family budget Nathan and I had made last year. That seemed like a whole lifetime ago. There was so much hope in that budget. We never once considered me losing a job. The reality I now faced seemed unthinkable a year ago. If only we had put more aside for a global pandemic. I took a deep breath and said a little prayer, just like my mother had taught me. "Please, dear God, help us find a way to survive with one salary."

Then I began chopping. First, I canceled our cable package. I ordered an antenna and signed up for more streaming services, hoping this would be enough. I also canceled yard service and my gym membership. The gym membership was a little redundant since the gym was closed. I had spoken with Grace several times, and I hoped at some point she would have an online class, but she hadn't figured that out yet. I scratched through the entertainment budget. What good is an entertainment budget when everything is closed? That nearly made me laugh. Nearly. We won't be going to Cardinals games, the theater, the movies, or even out to dinner with friends. Everything is closed. No nail salon or hairdresser. Even after I canceled everything we didn't need, we were still coming up short each month. I crossed off the clothes budget. Since the only thing I was wearing was sweats and exercise clothes, I hardly needed money for clothes. But the kids would still need summer things, as they were growing fast. I hoped I could find some deals at Costco or Sam's. That was all we could now afford. I had had about all the budgeting I could handle when the doorbell rang.

Adam greeted me with a big hug. "Hey, Sis, do you have a moment?" he asked.

"Sure, I need a break." I let him in as sounds of screaming came from the living room. "Just give me a minute," I said, pulling Oliver from Nathan's office by his shirt collar. "Maybe we could talk in the basement while Oliver plays with Legos," I said, giving Oliver my most severe look.

"That sounds fine," Adam replied tentatively. "OK with you, Oliver?"

Oliver just shrugged as I pulled him into the basement family room. Once settled, Adam began, "I've sold my house, Roni. Got a really good price. One thing doing well here is the housing market. Seems I hit it just right."

"That's great," I started.

"But," he broke in, "I have to be out of my house next week, and I don't have an apartment in Seattle yet and don't plan on moving until June. That sort of leaves me homeless for a month."

"Oh, what are you going to do?" I asked, with a strong suspicion I knew why he was here.

"Well, I was hoping you could help me out. I'd like to stay here for a month, and I need someplace to put some of my things for a while too."

"Oh, Adam, you know I'd like to help, but we're a little cramped ourselves with everyone home all day."

"What if we cleaned out the maid's room you have?" he asked "I bet it's mostly junk, and it would work just fine for me. I'd be happy to pay rent, since I'm sort of in the money," he added with a grin.

"I guess you know I lost my job," I said. "I hate the thought of charging my brother for living here, but the extra money would come in handy. It's actually an answer to a prayer. Let's take a look at the room."

Oliver was delighted to dig into the maid's room with us. Adam was right; it was mostly junk. Almost everything in there we could trash or donate to Goodwill.

"We'll have to talk to Nathan," I said.

"Talk to me about what?" Nathan asked, poking his head into the room.

"Oh, hi." Adam greeted Nathan with a handshake. "I was just asking Roni if I could rent this room for a month."

At Nathan's puzzled look, I spoke up, "Adam sold his house at a great profit and now has to vacate before he's ready to leave for Seattle. He has graciously offered to help us out with our budget problem if we can clean up this mess and make it livable."

"Let's start cleaning," Nathan said.

Cleaning out the maid's room was a great distraction. I listed a couple of items on craigslist. I got $200 for everything I'd listed to sell. Adam borrowed a truck from a friend, and we loaded up everything else and drove it to Goodwill. It took a little more than I expected to get the room clean. I hadn't given it much attention since we moved in. It turned out to be the perfect space for Adam. It was large enough for his queen-sized bed and his work computer. It also had an attached bathroom, which turned out to be quite nice when thoroughly scrubbed. In less than a week, Adam had moved in.

We saw very little of Adam except for meals. He was amazed that I was cooking. After weeks of watching Rachel Ray and Martha Stewart, I was starting to get the hang of it. It was fun having Adam around. The kids, especially Oliver, found him a much-needed distraction. I enjoyed helping him pick an apartment in Seattle. He found one on the eleventh floor with a view of the Space Needle. I would have loved to be planning the trip with him, but there was this whole pandemic thing preventing me from going anywhere.

I tried to make schedules for me and the kids to bring more structure to our days, but it was hard. My kids' school was making some progress with their "learn at home" program. They each had some lessons on Google, but it was sporadic and didn't always work. Katlin was frustrated when it didn't work, and Oliver was frustrated when it did. At times when he was supposed to be watching something on his iPad, he was more likely under the table or running away from the screen. Katlin was making a better effort but missed her friends terribly. She tried to talk to some of them on FaceTime, but the conversations didn't always go well. More often than not, the effort only made her sad. Clearly there was a "mean girls" dynamic happening. Sometimes her calls with them went well; sometimes they left her in tears. I hoped I could find a way to help her with this.

My parents came a couple of times that month to spend time with Adam before he left. I think we all were wondering how long it would be before we could see him again. In one of my mother's trips, she brought her gardening tools and boxes of vegetable plants.

"I've decided you need a garden," she announced. "Dad is going to run to Home Depot and buy a frame for a box garden and soil. It will be fun."

I deeply doubted that it would be fun, but it certainly was a distraction. It was hard work, and I had no confidence in my ability to make anything grow. The kids enjoyed playing in the dirt. We planted tomatoes, cucumbers, assorted peppers, and herbs. My mother gave me all kinds of directions for tending to the plants. Dad bought tomato cages and showed me how to install them in the garden. He even enclosed the garden in a green mesh material to keep out "critters." I never thought the cute rabbits and squirrels running through our yard were a threat. This was all a new and illuminating experience.

When it was all done, my mother and I stood and admired the effort. "I know that losing your job was hard for you," she told me. "I thought you needed a distraction. Working in the garden can be a great stress reliever. I hope it helps you. Plus, you'll have fresh produce all summer long."

I wanted to say something, but the big lump in my throat wouldn't let a word out. I gave her a big hug and kiss. Sometimes my mother did know just what I needed.

A week later, I was helping Adam pack for his big move when the doorbell rang. It was Megan. She looked totally disheveled. Her hair was long and unwashed. She was wearing what looked like yesterday's sweats, and her eyes were red and swollen.

"I need to see Nathan," she spurted, slurring her words.

"Megan, what's happened to you?" I stammered. "Are you drunk?"

71

"What's it to you? I don't have to be nice to you anymore. You fired me, you pig. I need to see Nathan. You can't keep me from him. He loves me."

I took in a deep breath. So many little clues were falling into place. All the odd comments she had made in the last six months were now as clear as a bell. I think I might actually have fallen backward, like I was punched in the gut. Adam came up behind me and helped me stand.

"Nathan," he shouted. "You're needed at the door now." He turned to me as Nathan came in the room and whispered, "I'm going to find the kids and take them out back to play."

I think I nodded. I felt like I was floating above the scene. My mind simply wasn't accepting what I saw and heard. Nathan saw Megan and dropped his head in his hands with a muffled sigh.

"Tell her you love me, Nathan," Megan shouted, slurring the words. "Tell her we ber- long to…to…together. You should move out and live with me."

Nathan faced Megan. "No, Megan. It was all a mistake. A terrible mistake. I told you it would never happen again. Weren't you listening? You need to go home and forget anything happened. I'm not leaving my family."

"But she betrayed you first. You should leave the bitch. She's trash."

"No, Megan. I don't care what Roni did. I love her, not you. Go home!"

"Ha," she spit out. "I've got no home. This bitch fired me so I'm living with my parents. I told them all about us too. They said I should sue your asses."

With that, the world, my broken world, came back into focus, and I found my voice. "For God's sake Megan, sue for what? Our company closed the office because, in case you didn't notice, there's a pandemic," I spurted out.

"You fired me because I was sleeping with your husband. He knows all about your boyfriend Dan. I told him you were sleeping around. How about that!" This time she actually did spit.

Now I saw myself falling into a hole. A nasty big hole. I didn't think I could stand much longer. All my lies and shame were spilling out into our street. Right in front of my house. My home. Nathan. My wonderful, loving Nathan. Was he as bad as me? Worse?

Nathan broke the silence and brought me back to reality. "Megan, I'm going to call you an Uber. You can leave your car in the street. You can't drive in this condition," Nathan told her as he slid his phone out of his pocket. "I'm going to send you back to your parents' house and hope we never see you again. Maybe your parents can come get the car tomorrow. Do you understand?"

"You're just saying that because she's standing there," Megan slurred. "You know I mean something to you."

"I think you're a very disturbed person," Nathan told her. "Maybe I should cancel the Uber and call your parents. What's their number?"

"No, I'll take your stupid Uber," she shouted. "And you'll never see me again. You're passing up the best thing you ever had."

The Uber came quickly. At least that was a blessing. Nathan saw her safely tucked into the car and told the driver to take her straight home. He said he was calling her parents to make sure she got home safely. I quickly searched through my Jonas work files and found a number for her parents. I called them and explained that Megan was going to need some help and support. I told them how she had appeared at our door. They were duly concerned and promised to take care of her.

Just to make sure they understood, I added, "I hope you know Megan lost her job because our office closed. Everyone who worked at Jonas lost their job, including me." I could tell from their response that this was not how Megan had presented the situation. I had to feel sorry for them. I had a daughter too. As I hung up, I turned around. Nathan was standing there.

"It was only twice," he blurted out. "I see now that she's not mentally stable. She said you were having an affair. I didn't want to believe her. I didn't believe her, but still the doubt… I—I wanted to punish you, I guess. You were always leaving. I was stupid. I'm so sorry." Suddenly I had a vision of me falling through the floor, down to what? Hell? Wonderland? Something that wasn't real. This wasn't real, was it? This is something that happens in a soap opera, not to me. But it was happening. Nathan was standing in front of me with sad red eyes. I couldn't let him keep wondering. I knew, from the depths of my soul, whatever it cost, I had to tell him the truth. The awful, painful truth.

Just then, Adam poked his head in the door. He could see by the expression of sheer horror on our faces that we needed some time.

"How about I take the kids and drive through McDonald's and find a picnic table to eat at?" he asked.

"Good idea," Nathan told him. My words weren't coming out, but tears were streaming down my face. I was hurt, but I wasn't mad at Nathan. I was mad at me. Stupid me.

When Adam and the kids left, Nathan and I sat on the living room floor facing each other.

"I should be really furious with you, but how can I be? She wasn't completely wrong about me," I told him through the tears. "A couple of times, when I was on a trip, I…I…I made terrible mistakes." These were the most difficult words I had ever spoken. Words that could destroy my life. My family's life. What was I thinking with Dan? How terribly reckless I had been. Now that the proverbial shoe was on the other foot, I could clearly see the harm I had done. At that moment, I knew Dan meant nothing to me. Nathan meant everything. My family meant everything. Even if I wasn't any good at being a wife or mother, I would trade all my business talent for this family. Surely there must be a way out of this dreadful hole I've dug us into. "Oh, God, please help me find a way out of this mess," I prayed.

"Well, this is a pretty mess. I kept telling myself she was wrong," Nathan said. "Why? Do you love me? Are you in love with someone else?"

"Oh, God, Nathan, I wish with all my heart I could tell you why. I haven't been able to answer that for myself, but the one thing I do know—I know as well as I know anything in life—is I love you and only you. I always have. I think, maybe I just got so full of myself, my business power—the trials of having a career and family—I don't know. I really, truly don't know."

"Are you ever going to see him again?" he asked.

"No, never," I answered. "Are you ever going to see her again?"

"Absolutely, most definitely, emphatically not," he answered.

"What now?" I wanted to know.

"I don't know," he said honestly. "You hurt me, Roni. I'm furious, in fact. But I know my behavior doesn't give me much ground to stand on. Still, I don't know how to put it past me. Do you want to split up?"

"No, no, no, no." I started crying again. "I love you, Nathan."

"Perhaps we need some time apart or counseling," he suggested.

"Anything you say," I said. "I'll do anything it takes to heal us."

I reached for his hand, but he pulled it away and stepped back. "Not right now," he whispered as he turned and walked away. I couldn't imagine a way forward, a way to healing. But somehow, in this darkest of moments, I thought there must be a way to make this OK. I had to find a way to heal us. I would fight for this marriage as I never did before. It may take a long time. Maybe not today or tomorrow, but we would be OK. We had to be OK. II had to make it work. Whatever it took, I would make it work.

Adam returned with the kids a little while later. I was still sitting on the living room floor, staring at the carpet, eyes red from crying.

"Everything, OK, Roni?" he asked.

"No, it's not," I said honestly. "It may never be again, but I'm going to try with everything I have to make it better."

"I didn't think Nathan—" Adam started.

"No, Adam, don't blame Nathan, I'm just as much to blame, maybe more. I can't explain. I don't want to explain. It's just too hard. I'd rather not say anything to our parents yet."

"Of course, Roni. Whatever you need."

Nathan slept in the guest room that night and for the rest of the month. We were both rather cool to each other. Frigid, actually. Nathan had trouble even looking at me. Adam was at most meals, and he kept the conversation at least civil. He has a great sense of humor, which he could use to diffuse almost any situation. That's why he was so good at his job. I said a little prayer of thanks that Adam was here. Was God listening to my prayer? Was Adam an answer to one or many of them? Did God know I needed him more than I did? Perhaps my mother was right. Perhaps I needed to pray more. I can't imagine how much worse it would have been if Adam wasn't here. Without the virus, I expect Nathan would have moved out. But now, where could he go? Most hotels were closed. Even if they weren't, we were barely making it on one salary. No extra money in the budget for a separation.

Katlin's birthday was May 27, a Wednesday. I invited my parents to come down for a couple of days to celebrate Katlin's birthday and say goodbye to Adam. He was leaving Saturday. Last year for Katlin's birthday we had a bounce house, clowns, and face painters in our yard with twenty-five kids and their parents. It was catered, and we had a magnificent cake in the shape of a castle. All arranged by Megan. Ugh, Megan. Clearly none of that was happening this year. Because of the virus rules, we couldn't have more than ten people in one place. Most of Katlin's schoolmates were staying strictly at home, as were we. Her party would be a simple cake I made with Martha's help (Martha Stewart, that is), her favorite spaghetti and cheesy bread, all safely eaten outside with Adam and my parents. I got some festive balloons from the Dollar Store (my new favorite store) and some party favors. I had actually talked to Katlin about what she wanted, which included a long list of accessories for her American Girl doll. I ordered them online and wrapped them colorfully. After dinner, I had arranged a joint parade for Katlin and Adam. As soon as dinner was over, we went to our front porch and watched as fifteen cars led by the local fire department came down our street with balloons and banners. My sister Korie and her family stopped for a bit. They brought Katlin a great art kit. Some of Katlin's friends came and some of Adam's. It was a lovely parade but created too much distance with the people we cared about. When everything was cleaned up, I went upstairs to tuck Katlin into bed and found her crying.

"Oh, sweetheart, what's wrong? Didn't you like your birthday party?" I asked.

"It's not your fault. I know you tried," she sobbed. "But I couldn't have friends over. It wasn't like last year. I miss my friends. I miss having a big party."

"I know you do. I'm so very sorry," I told her with tears in my eyes. This was hard enough for adults. It's so much worse for children. I felt helpless. "Didn't you like the parade?"

"It was very nice, but seeing some friends and not being able to play with them is so hard. When will we get back to normal? When will I be able to play with friends?"

"I don't have any answers," I said. "But I know with all my heart that it will happen. Maybe we could focus on the good things we have, like this lovely house, wonderful grandparents, and plenty of food to eat. I've been praying much more. It has helped me. You should try to thank God for the things you have and ask for what you need. He's great to talk to."

"Thanks, Mom," she said with a shy smile. "I'm going to thank God that you learned to cook. Dinner was great, and the cake was wonderful." I held her until she fell asleep and quietly prayed that what I'd told her was the truth. Then I slipped into bed with Nathan, who had moved back into our room while my parents were here. It felt so good to have him near, but I didn't expect it to last.

Saturday morning at the crack of dawn, we all watched as Adam drove his SUV off to Seattle packed to the roof with all his worldly goods. The trip was over 1,700 miles and would take more than two days. It was a clear day, and he made terrific progress. By nightfall, he sent us pictures of himself in front of Mt. Rushmore. A day and a half later, he was in his new apartment in Seattle. I was happy for him, but it felt like another big empty space in my life. After my parents left, Nathan moved into the maid's room Adam had vacated. He seemed further away than ever. He got up early each morning and made the bed, hoping the kids didn't notice. He tried to act normal. The kids may have noticed something, but so much was different I think they just thought this was all a part of the pandemic. We were all searching for a new normal. Just like that, May was over.

By the end of May, the U.S. had recorded more than 100,000 deaths due to the virus, with 1,800,000 confirmed cases. Our world was mostly locked down to prevent the spread of the virus. Restaurants and all entertainment or hospitality venues were closed to the public. If we wanted food from somewhere other than our kitchen, we had to order online and pick it up from the curb or have it delivered. No one traveled. No one went out except to the grocery store and only with a mask. Many people like me lost jobs. Single mothers couldn't work because they had no school or day care for their children. The pandemic had crippled our lives.

As if a global pandemic weren't enough to deal with, in Minneapolis, an African American man named George Perry Floyd, Jr., was murdered by a police officer during an arrest for a suspected counterfeit twenty-dollar bill. The officer, Derek Chauvin, one of four police officers who arrived on the scene, knelt on Floyd's neck and back for nine minutes and twenty-nine seconds while a crowd, including children, watched. The scene was recorded by a young girl in the crowd and played over and over again on national TV. As Mr. Floyd was dying, he cried, "I can't breathe." These words became a rallying cry against police brutality, especially against people of color. Protests, mostly peaceful, quickly spread across the United States and the world. While the majority of the protests were peaceful, some escalated into riots, looting, and street skirmishes with police. Some 200 cities in the U.S. imposed curfews by early June. I suspected the debate over racial injustice that began in May would continue for a very long time. Probably long past the pandemic.

Like most of my friends, I had a hard time moving past the horrific image I saw over and over again on TV of Officer Chauvin murdering George Floyd. This certainly wasn't the first case of police brutality against a person of color, but somehow, for many of us it became more personal. This just couldn't be ignored. Like many of my neighbors, I demonstrated my feelings by posting a "Black Lives Matter" sign in my front yard. I noticed Black Lives Matters vigils being held around our neighborhood, on the steps of city hall, at busy intersections and local churches. I wanted to do something. My heart was so full of rage, I HAD to do something. I was delighted when my neighbor, Rebecca, invited me to a peaceful vigil in front of a local church. We purchased another "Black Lives Matter" sign from the Novel Neighbor, a local bookstore. We assembled in front of the local church just before 6:00 pm. The leader asked us to kneel on one knee in prayer for nine minutes and 29 second, the same amount of time that Officer Chauvin knelt on George Floyd's neck, slowly killing him. As I prayed my mind was filled with centuries of atrocities inflicted on people of color from slavery, to lynchings to segregation to endless police brutality. I prayed that it would all end, that we could begin to see each other with love. Tears were streaming down my face. My knee hurt so bad I had to change knees. When the time had passed, we rose and stood silently along the street holding our signs. I just couldn't stop the tears. Rebecca and I walked home in silence. I will forever be glad I attended this vigil and I won't forget.

# June 2020 –
# Summer Without Fun

In June, I picked up my calendar, knowing what I would see. A Jonas meeting had been scheduled in New York this month to review plans for the next month's Olympics. And the second week of June was marked for a family vacation. Both kids were scheduled to go to camp at the end of June. There would be no meeting. No Olympics, no family vacation, no camp. Camp had closed for the summer. There wasn't even a family. Since Nathan had moved into the maid's quarters, I seldom saw him.

School, what there was of it, was finally out and so was the sun. But we only felt gloom. To add to our despair, Oliver's teacher had told us he was way behind his class in reading. He would need summer school before he could enter first grade. That was fine except there was no school. Somehow, they planned to do this remotely on the computer with a reading specialist from the Special School District. Earlier in the year, when Anna was still in control of things, Oliver had been tested because of his reading problems and qualified for help from a resource teacher. However, it never materialized because the school shut down. The reading specialist had tried to work with Oliver via the computer, but it wasn't working. I had no idea how I would get him to sit still at a tablet for a lesson. He knew he had trouble reading and had decided he couldn't do it, although he was pretty good at memorizing sight words and could read more than he thought he could. But if he didn't know the word, he had no tools to sound it out. I had little time to worry about this because I had more trouble keeping both kids out of Nathan's office space. With school officially out, all efforts at a schedule had collapsed, and the kids ran rampant throughout the house.

"This isn't working!" screamed Nathan when yet another meeting was interrupted by the kids' fighting. "I have to have quiet to work. I'm on calls all day long. I can't possibly work with this noise. We have to do something now!" he demanded.

"I'm completely out of ideas," I shouted back. "What do you want me to do? Tie them up?"

"I wouldn't mind it today," he said, sinking into his chair. "Maybe we could move my office."

"To where?" I asked. "You're living in the maid's quarters. That's the most likely space."

"Yes, and you know why," he snapped.

"Don't shout," Katlin cried. "I'm sorry I was loud."

I rushed to her side. "It's not your fault. You're a kid with nothing to do. Your dad didn't mean it, right?" I said, looking hard at Nathan.

"No, of course, sweetie. I didn't want to make you cry. But I do need silence to work."

"You can have my bedroom," offered Oliver. "I'll sleep in a tent outside. That would be fun."

"That's it!" I shouted. "Oliver, you have a great idea."

"Oliver's not sleeping outside," Nathan barked.

"Not Oliver's room, but the guest bedroom. We could make that spare room into an office. It's at the end of the hall and it has—wait for it—"

"A *door!*" Nathan finished the sentence for me with great excitement.

"Why didn't we think of this before? It's perfect," I said.

"Maybe because the guest room is full of furniture we'll have to move? Isn't that why Adam didn't stay there? It's not an obvious choice considering that."

"Yes, yes, but we can do this. Look how well we cleaned out the maid's room. We'll do this even faster. We can put the bed in a corner of the basement—the unfinished part. I think we can work around the dresser," I said excitedly. I was glad to have a project.

We put the plan into action immediately. We moved everything that we could out of the room. Nathan left the desk where it was in the living room, partly because it was much too large for the new office and partly because it gave me a space to work with Oliver. He found a perfect desk online with a chair and a file cabinet. We decided to paint the room a color more suitable for an office. Everybody got to help. By the week's end, Nathan had a real office with a priceless door. We also set up major consequences for entering Daddy's office uninvited. I made homemade pizza to celebrate. For a few precious days, we were all working toward a common goal, like a real family. Maybe, just maybe, we could do this.

Each night as I lay in bed alone, I prayed for a way back to Nathan, to repair our family. More often than not, I cried myself to sleep. I hated myself. Forgiving Nathan was much easier than forgiving myself.

I spent as much time as possible outside with the kids. The parks were open but not the playgrounds or the pools or the bathrooms, which made going to the park not so fun. That didn't leave us much. We needed more to do. I called my Aunt Mary, who lived on ten acres at the edge of St. Louis County. She had a lovely home and an even more lovely pool. She also had an Olympic-sized trampoline where her eight grandchildren often played. Social distancing required us to stay away from the rest of the family, but I asked if we could come when no one else was there. She was delighted for us to come in the middle of the week when all her family was at work. Katlin, Oliver, and I drove out to Aunt Mary's farm for the best day we'd had in months. I promised to stay outside as much as possible. For lunch, I grilled hot dogs for us all. We took a long walk along the creek behind her house. Both kids got so muddy I had to hose them down before they could get back in the pool. They found all sorts of fossils in the creek, which we carried home at the end of the day. But mostly we swam. Both kids swam the length of the pool over and over, jumping in repeatedly. We drove home exhausted, but it was a peaceful exhaustion. The kind you feel at the end of a pleasant and active day. This was what we'd been missing: being together, out of the house, and having fun. I don't think I could ever repay Aunt Mary for this gift.

When we got home, the kids had many stories to tell their dad. After a quick dinner and thorough bath, they fell asleep. For once, there was no arguing, no fighting, no begging them to go to sleep. They were sound asleep as soon as they hit the pillow.

I opened a bottle of wine and asked Nathan to join me on the couch. Handing him a glass, I said, "I wish you could have been there. It was so much fun and so relaxing. We need more family time like that. Do you think you could get a day off and come with us?"

"I'd like that. I'd like to be a family again, but the wounds are still raw."

"I know," I agreed. "We have to do something to find our way back. You do want that, don't you?

"I do, but it's so hard. Forgetting is harder than forgiving."

"I understand. It's hard for me too. I miss you. But a journey of a million miles starts with one step, right?" I offered.

"One step," he smiled. "I'll look for a weekday I can take off, and we'll all go to Aunt Mary's for a day."

We had our family day a week later. The kids took Nathan to the creek and showed him the swimming hole and the old fallen tree. They even found a turtle swimming. We basked in the sun, ate hamburgers off the grill, and munched on watermelon for dessert. The sky was so blue I thought God had painted it just for us. It was a perfect day, like the peace in the eye of a storm. I told Aunt Mary she could charge a lot of money for a vacation day. She smiled. "That would be work," she replied. "Having family is fun." Before we left, I gave her a gift certificate to her favorite store. It wasn't much compared to what our time here was worth, but it was something.

We managed to limp to the end of June. Oliver had reading lessons on Zoom now. It was a battle, but not as hard as before. Katlin was reading and talking on the phone with friends. We were adjusting to a masked-up, social-distanced life in a pandemic, but it was far, far from over.

On June 30, more than 2,600,000 cases and 120,000 deaths had been reported in the U.S. Florida and South Carolina broke single-day records for new cases as infection levels for Missouri reached new highs. It was time for June to be over.

# July 2020 –
# Learning to Celebrate Safely

I stopped looking at my calendar. (Actually, I threw the damn thing out.) This should have been the month of the 2020 Olympics, but there were no 2020 Olympics. As hard as that was for me, I couldn't imagine how hard it must be for the athletes who'd spent their whole lives preparing for this moment…only to have no moment. Maybe in 2021. We could only hope and pray. We needed more prayer. My mother was right about that. As the holiday approached, I had no idea how much prayer we would need by the end of the month.

My parents loved the Fourth of July. They loved every holiday. My mother even found a way to make Groundhog's Day special. For the Fourth, she invited us and my sister's family to come spend the day at their house. Last year we spent the day at a fair in St. Charles with another family and saw an amazing fireworks display. This year there'd be no fairs and no fireworks displays. So, my mother's offer seemed like a big boost. I ordered some yard games online (how would we ever have survived a pandemic without the internet?) and made red, white, and blue cupcakes (thanks again, Martha!). The single servings were virus safe since no one needed to handle one but the eater.

We drove to Washington midmorning. Katlin and Oliver had a great time playing in the big backyard with their cousins James and Henry. Experts recommended we avoid shared foods during the pandemic, like a bowl of anything, and find single-serve party food, like kabobs.

My mother got a little kabob-happy. She made her amazing steak shish kabobs for the grown-ups and hot dog kabobs for the kids. She's so clever. We also had fruit kabobs. Korie brought potato chips in individual bags. It wasn't as good as her potato casserole, but it was safer. As soon as the sun went down, my dad set off a spectacular fireworks display. The kids celebrated with sparklers. It was way past everyone's bedtime when we drove home. The kids fell asleep pretty quickly, and Nathan and I were as silent as if we were sleeping—well, maybe more silent. He snores. But then I only hear him when we sleep in the same room. We hadn't done that since the hurricane named Megan, with the exception of the nights my parents stayed with us. Or should I say the tsunami named...me?

Tonight's silence was something different. During dinner, my father had announced he was going to be working at Washington's Mercy Hospital with virus patients. I think we all took a collective gasp. He was sixty-seven, and it was way too dangerous for a man his age to be so closely exposed to the virus. As if that weren't enough, Korie said she was "on call" to work with virus patients at her hospital.

"The need isn't overwhelming right now, but they expect it will be worse soon. If I do work with virus patients, I'm going to stay at Geoff's parents' house, and they will stay with Geoff and the kids. I don't want to risk infecting any of them," Korie told us.

"I'm going to sleep in our camper," Dad announced. "I couldn't live with myself if I infected your mother." She gave him such a loving look, it tugged at my heart. They were both so brave, my heart swelled.

"I might join you at your Aunt Mary's the next time you go out there," my mother told me. "If your dad is going to be at the hospital, I'll need a distraction. Mary said I could stay there a couple of days. It sounds like fun."

The following week, we had another great day at Aunt Mary's. My mother swam with the kids, and we all sat and talked. She made delicious individual mac and cheese casseroles for lunch with chocolate cupcakes for dessert. To top it off, she brought out homemade popsicles for our afternoon snack. If I knew my mother, there was kale in those tasty popsicles. That was so Mom. The kids devoured everything she made. But the day was marred by a thunderstorm that popped up and put an end to our fun. Since we had agreed to stay outside, there was nothing to do in the rain but go home, putting a damper on all our spirits.

I didn't feel like I was making any progress in repairing my marriage or teaching Oliver or helping Katlin navigate the trials of friendship. I certainly wasn't making any progress in my career, which seemed dead in the water. I wasn't making any progress on anything except cooking. Our evening meals had vastly improved. Often, they were whatever Rachel Ray had cooked on her show the day before, but I had ordered several cookbooks and I was making real progress through them. I not only cooked for dinner but also breakfast and lunch. Before the pandemic, we never had breakfast or lunch together unless it was a special occasion at a restaurant. Breakfast had always been a bowl of cereal. Now we had bacon and eggs—not just eggs, but omelets. Or pancakes. I actually made pancakes from scratch. I even made chicken soup for lunch. Of course, this took a lot of my time, and I was ignoring the house. My ability to keep the house clean, especially with all of us home all day, was less encouraging.

"Roni, this place looks like a pigsty," Nathan shouted. I had to admit, it was pretty bad, but shouting didn't help. "You have nothing to do but take care of the kids and keep the house clean. I know that you're not used to homemaker work, but could you try a little more?"

I think steam was actually coming straight out of my head, "That's so unfair," I shouted back. "In case you haven't noticed, I'm making three meals a day for four people. THREE," I shouted. "And I'm helping Oliver with his reading and Katlin with…with…with just being in a bummer summer. And, if you haven't noticed, I've mowed the lawn when you're too busy. I think you could cut me a little slack."

"Whatever," he snorted. "Clean this up."

Never, never in all the years of our marriage had Nathan shouted at me like that. Never. I thought things were getting a little better, but clearly not. I didn't think this was about our messy house. (Well, maybe a little.) I think it was about our messy life. The mistakes I had made. The mistakes he had made. Some wounds were hard to heal. This wasn't going to happen overnight. Just the same, I did clean up the house, but we had hot dogs for dinner.

I didn't have an easy fix for my marriage, but I knew I had to do something about this miserable, safely social-distanced summer. I spent my whole career in travel. Surely I could find a way to take a virus-safe trip with my family. I searched the web for ideas: Take a walk, go camping, stay in your own motor home. Not helpful. All the websites said to avoid air travel and go somewhere you can drive to in a day. Stay out of hotels or anyplace you are sharing space with others, including restaurants. We weren't a camping family, and I couldn't imagine us in an RV. I thought about this for two days when it hit me. We could rent a house with a kitchen somewhere with beautiful scenery and lots of fun things to do outside, away from people. Some place on the water; any kind of water would add to the activities we could do. Living in St. Louis, this would be a challenge. It wasn't a perfect idea. I didn't know how the kids would react. But it was something. I read once that Winston Churchill said, "A change is as good as a rest." We needed a change and a rest.

I took out an old map and looked at options a day's drive away. The Ozarks were close, as was Branson, but the virus was running wild there. Across the state was Kansas. Nothing there. Or Oklahoma. Arkansas had lovely rivers, but it also had a high infection rate. I wanted to avoid that. Then I saw it: Kentucky Lake. It's beautiful. There would be tons of lake things to do, and it's just a little over 200 miles away. Far enough for a change. Not so far that we can't easily drive there in a day. Now all I had to do was find a house on the lake with a dock and a boat. Easy, right?

It turned out to be easier than I'd thought. I still had some connections. I called a company that I knew rented homes. After a couple of referrals and a few wrong turns, I found the perfect house on Kentucky Lake. The house had a dock, a boat, and two wave runners. Perfect. It wasn't cheap, but we had no airfare or car rental, and we would make most of our own meals. After dinner that night, I proposed the idea to the whole family.

"Yay, vacation!" Oliver cried.

"It sounds amazing," Katlin added. "It's not the ocean, but it's something. Good job, Mom." Did my daughter actually give me a "good job"? I might faint.

"Can I drive a wave runner?" asked Oliver with much more excitement than I'd anticipated.

"Wait just a minute," Nathan said. "I think your mom and I have to talk about this. You know, money is tight. We need to figure out if we can afford it."

"Come on, Dad," Oliver and Katlin cried together.

"We'll talk again tomorrow," Nathan announced. "Off to bed. No crying or the deal is dead now."

When they started to complain, he stared them down. "Off to bed. Now!"

While Nathan was helping the kids to bed, I mixed my best margaritas. Nathan loved margaritas. Surely this would help.

When he came downstairs, I handed him a shimmering cocktail.

"Don't think you can get me drunk so I agree to your scheme," he said, taking the cocktail.

"The thought never crossed my mind," I said innocently. "But I suppose you're going to tell me why you don't approve of my vacation idea."

He took a long sip. "I know what you're doing. I can read your mind. You think a family vacation will solve all our problems."

"I know our problems won't be solved that easily. But you have to admit, even with our wonderful outings to Aunt Mary's, we need a vacation. We all need to get out of this house, out of this city, and away from our routine—or lack thereof. After all, that's what I sold for all those years."

"I don't like how you blindsided me by including the kids in your pronouncement."

"Maybe that was a little subversive," I admitted. "I did want to see how they would react to the idea. And I was pretty sure you'd nix it without discussion. Is the idea of spending a week away with me—with us—so horrible?

He drained his drink and set the glass down. "A year ago, I would have loved the idea. We had so much less baggage a year ago. I don't want to feel like this, but I can't get past the lies and deception. I don't know how."

My eyes were filling with tears. I said a quiet prayer for the right words. "Look, first of all, we owe it to the kids to try and give them some summer fun, a break from our shelter-in-place. This hasn't been easy for them either. They aren't to blame for any of this—the virus, the school closing, our problems." I took a deep breath, willing myself to continue. "I don't want to trivialize my faults, which I know are gargantuan, but there are faults on both sides. I think we had problems before too. They just weren't so obvious. The one thing I'm sure of is that we aren't making progress on any front staying here, being mad or whatever. Isn't this worth a try? Aren't *we* worth a try? Not just you and me, but our family? Besides, don't you need a break? You've been working so hard." Now the tears were flowing freely.

Nathan turned away. I know he hates it when I cry, but I couldn't help it. "You make good points, especially about the kids. I know I've been a bear... I just have so much anger, I don't know what to do with it. I'll give this a try, but in separate bedrooms."

"That's why I got a four-bedroom house," I said. I didn't want separate bedrooms, but I wasn't going to push. "I hope you can leave some of your anger at home and really give this try."

He didn't answer but at least we were going on vacation. Yay!!

I managed to get a reservation for the last week of July. We would leave on Friday, right after Oliver's last reading lesson for the summer, and return the following Friday. Last year school started the second week of August, but our school had no plans for returning yet. I wondered if they would have school at all. All these worries we would put behind us for one blissful week. At least that was the plan. As we planned to mostly eat in the rental house, I was busy preparing meals for our trip. I froze a ton of spaghetti sauce in ziplock bags as well as taco meat and soup. I made bags of pancake mix and coffee cake mix. They would only need the wet ingredients to finish. I made chocolate chip cookie dough and froze it. I bought everything that I thought we would need in our vacation home: toilet paper, paper towels, paper plates and cups, and disinfectant by the gallon. I found a few water toys. They were hard to come by—another pandemic shortage. I packed games and toys for the kids and books for me. I made sure we had copious amounts of bug spray, suntan lotion, and hand sanitizer. We would also need laundry and dish detergent. I bought hot dogs, hamburgers, and steaks to make on the provided gas grill. And, of course, what summer outing would be complete without s'mores? When the day for our departure came, our Escalade was packed to the roof.

"Are you sure this is a vacation?" Nathan asked as he looked at the pile in the SUV. "It looks more like a work-cation to me." He wasn't wrong. Our vacations usually involved very little work on our part other than showing up at a hotel and restaurant. This was certainly different.

"It's a 2020 vacation," I replied. "By definition, that makes it a work-cation."

As we drove off, I said, "The trip should take about four hours, depending on stops." We left late morning. I thought a drive-through lunch about an hour in might break up the trip. Taking a tip from a mom's vacation book, I hid a couple of little gifts in the car. They were designed to be activities the kids could do in the car. We drove through a McDonald's. Katlin immediately spilled her juice, and Nathan squirted catsup all over himself. That prompted a stop at a gas station, which necessitated lots of disinfecting. Another hour in, the kids had lost interest in the gifts and were glued to their tablets playing games I don't usually allow. Then another bathroom stop and more disinfecting. We finally reached our destination at about 5:30. Not bad, everything considered.

Perched right on the lake with a serviceable dock, the house was every bit as inviting as it appeared online. I asked Nathan to take the kids for a little walk while I went inside to disinfect everything. I had brought our own sheets and towels—no small packing feat—and changed the beds. My family returned just as I had finished scrubbing and helped me unpack the car. We had noticed a pizza place as we drove in, and our hosts had thoughtfully left a menu on the table. We ordered a pizza and had it delivered. One vacation day down successfully. Six more to go.

Everybody wanted to start the next day with boating. The boat was a simple flat-bottomed boat that came equipped with a motor and life jackets.

"Kentucky Lake has over 2,000 miles of shoreline. It was created in 1944 by the construction of a dam, the Kentucky Dam, on the Tennessee River. It provides hydro-elec—"

"Enough, enough!" shouted Nathan over the roar of the motor. I had been reading from my research notes about the area. "We're not one of your tour groups. You're on vacation." He and the kids were laughing to the point of tears.

"No more education, Mom," pleaded Katlin. "This is vacation. We don't want to learn anything."

I held my notes up in the air and let go. As they whirled away in the wind, my fears subsided and I began to relax and enjoy the scenery. It was lovely. We had a wonderful day, topped off with grilled hamburgers and s'mores. True, it was more work than most vacations, but it was also more togetherness. As we sat in the comfortable modern living room playing games, I thought it just couldn't get any better. Last year, we had gone to a resort in Arizona. It was chic and expensive. I picked it because it had separate activities for the kids. I hardly saw them at all. We had feasted on steak and lobster in quiet candlelit restaurants. This was so much better. We were really, really together.

We hiked. We swam. We raced in the wave runners—Katlin and I on one, and Nathan and Oliver on the other. We sat on the deck and played games or watched the sunset or did nothing at all. We didn't go to the amusement park or even miniature golf. We ate the same foods I had been making at home, but it all tasted better. Maybe because we were exhausted and hungry from the day's activities. Maybe because it was someplace different. We stayed in our rented house and enjoyed one another's company. It felt like our house, but different. Not better or worse, just different. That was its key feature. Somewhere new.

Nathan and I had some nice talks on the deck after the kids went to bed. Not about anything big. We ignored the elephant in the room, the two people we had let invade our lives. But we talked about politics (boy, was there ever a lot to discuss there), about what I might do in the future, about our favorite movies or music, or about nothing at all. Once we even kissed. I was ready to return to our married life and leave the past behind us, but Nathan wasn't yet. The wounds were still too fresh.

Our time was over on Friday, and we sadly packed all our gear, minus the mountain of food we had eaten, into our Escalade and headed for St. Louis. The sun shone a little brighter going home. The kids were kinder to each other. We were all full of smiles.

Then the phone rang.

It was my mother. She told us that my father had contracted the virus. He had been sick for about four days. At first it seemed he would sail right through it, but then he got sicker and sicker. When his breathing had become strained, she called the ambulance today and he was taken to the hospital. To keep her safe, he had insisted she stay with a neighbor, but she checked on him nearly hourly. He had been admitted to the hospital, but no one was allowed to visit. All we could do was pray. I asked the family to bow their heads, and we all prayed for Grandpa.

By July 31, the U.S. registered 4,500,000 cases of the virus. On that day, almost 56,000 people were in a hospital fighting for their lives. One of them was my beloved father. So far in the U.S., 146,000 people had died due to the virus. I prayed my father would not be one.

# August 2020 –
# A Dark Cloud Building

August should have been a happy month. Baseball was back and the sun was out. But the St. Louis Cardinals team was sidelined after several players tested positive for the virus. The players who did not test positive had to quarantine in their hotel rooms in Milwaukee. They would miss nineteen days of their schedule. Baseball was sorely missed in a huge baseball town like St. Louis.

But baseball was the least of our worries. My poor mother was beside herself. My father was in the hospital fighting for his life against this virus we still knew so little about. If it were any other disease, Mom would have been right by his side, as would me and Korie. But this was all different. No one, not even a beloved spouse, was allowed to visit the virus patients. The only way Mom could see Dad was on FaceTime. Mostly the nurse just held the phone as he lay sleeping. I couldn't let my mother suffer alone. After nearly a week of her walking the floor in worry, calling the nurses every hour, I decided it would be better for her to wait for news with us, at our house. When I first proposed the plan to Nathan, he was less than enthusiastic.

"Where do you plan on her staying and for how long?" he asked.

I knew he knew the answer. With our guest room turned into his office and the maid's quarters now his domain, there were few options.

I wasn't going to say what he expected me to say. "Well, let's see what our options are," I began. "We could put both kids in one room."

"You know that won't work. Not even for one night," Nathan countered.

Of course, I knew it wouldn't work, but it seemed we had to look at the options one by one. Neither of us was going to state the obvious solution. I certainly wasn't leading with that.

"Or," I continued, "Mom could sleep with me in our king-sized bed."

"That's absurd. What would you say when she asked why I wasn't sleeping there?" he argued.

"Or," I went on without comment, "you could either move your office into the maid's quarters with you or you could move yourself to your office or…"

"I could move back into our bedroom," he finished. "I suppose that was your plan all along."

"Look, Nathan. Nothing about this is what I planned. I didn't plan on my father getting the virus. I didn't plan on us living in separate parts of the house for this long. I can't undo anything that was done in the past. I only know my sweet mother is in agony. Adam is in Seattle. Korie is working in a hospital, struggling to keep her family together. I want to do this for my mother, and the answer to your question is no. No, I don't want to tell her we're living in different parts of the house. I think she has enough to deal with right now. So, what do you think is the solution?"

"You knew when you brought it up that the only solution would be me moving back into our bedroom."

"Would that be so terrible? I'm not asking for a return to everything we had in the past. Maybe we can't get that back. But I want to help my mother through the hardest season of her life. What if Dad doesn't make it? Do you want her to get that news all alone in that house? Do you?"

Silence.

"I suppose I could take the kids and move in with her. Who knows when school will start again? I think the kids would be happy with that.

That's the only other solution I have." More silence. Minutes passed that seemed like hours.

"The virus infection rate is very high in Washington. People there are refusing to wear masks. God only knows why. They think wearing a mask violates their constitutional rights. Why or how totally baffles me. Nobody wants to wear a damn mask, but if it helps protect us against the virus, even a little, why not?" I was babbling now just to fill the silence.

"OK. Your mom can come here. I'll sleep in the master bedroom. But it doesn't mean I'm ready to be together," he said at last, as I knew he would. He was still my darling Nathan. He had just covered himself in a coat of anger. Little by little, the coat was getting thinner.

At first, my mother was unsure about the idea. She didn't want to be that far away from Dad. But she was tired of worrying by herself. She wanted family around her. She insisted on getting tested for the virus before she came. The testing proved to be a bigger trial than she'd anticipated. She called me in a state of extreme frustration.

"Roni, I can't figure out how to get a test," she sobbed. "I've seen pictures on the news of hour-long lines for the blasted test. I just couldn't do that." I knew it was bad when she invoked the near-swear "blasted." "I called the hospital, but they said I have to fill out an online form, and I just can't figure it out. There's no one to help me, and I can't get a test without that blasted form." There it was again—*blasted*. Poor mom.

"Where do you want to get the test?" I asked.

"Mercy has a clinic nearby that gives tests, if I ever figure this thing out."

"Let me find the form and fill it out for you. OK?" I said calmly.

"Oh, Roni, that would be a big help. My brain doesn't seem to be working very well just now."

"It's OK, Mom. I'll take care of it." I should have tried to find the necessary form before I spoke so confidently. It wasn't easy. I can't imagine how a person not used to navigating the internet would ever find the right one. I had to call Mom to get some insurance information and other details from her, but together, we managed to complete all the questions. Shortly after I completed the form, I got a notice that Mom's test was scheduled for 1:00 that afternoon. At 1:30, she called.

"Whatever you did Roni, it worked like magic. I went to the clinic, and they had me all signed in. But the test was really nasty. They stuck a long swab up my nose and rooted around like they were trying to hit my brain! I hope I never have to do that again." I did too. It took two days for her to get the results. Her test was negative. Praise God. No virus for my mother. Not yet, anyway.

Once she was confirmed negative, she agreed to come. I went alone to limit any exposure to the kids. When I drove up to the house, she ran out to greet me. We hugged and cried. I loaded up her mountain of supplies in short order. Before we drove to Willow Glen, we first drove to the hospital. Even though I knew we couldn't go in, we just wanted to be where he was for a little while. We sat in the car and prayed and cried.

When we got home, the kids were very glad to see her. They hugged her, and more tears were shed. I felt like I could hardly cry anymore. My mother busied herself by puttering in my garden. I was surprised at how much she found to do in our small yard. There were bushes and trees to trim and plants to water and endless weeding. None of that I had ever done, but I enjoyed watching her work. It was good to be outside, and the kids were enjoying the outdoors. I put sprinklers on to water the kids. My mother showed us how to make a water slide in the yard.

With the help of a nurse, we talked to Dad through FaceTime every day. Even if he was not awake, the nurse let us "see" him. Sometimes we did that a couple of times a day. Then we got the call that Dad's condition had worsened, and they were putting him on a ventilator. That was beyond hard to hear. If only we could see him in person. If only we could tell him how much we loved him. The sweet nurse put the phone to his ear and Mom spoke to him, so soothingly. My brain said he wasn't hearing, but my heart hoped he did. Adam also tried to talk with him through the nurse, as did Korie. But Korie was fighting her own battles. She had been called into work in the ER at St. Mary's. Her husband and her kids were staying with his parents to keep them safe in case she contracted the virus. She talked to Dad a couple of times, but as hospitalizations were rising, she was working around the clock. We prayed for her too. My mother's pastor from Washington came to visit. He was sweet and gave her as much comfort as possible. He made a wonderful suggestion that we attend services at a local church that was doing a great job of virtual services. We could all watch together on YouTube. It was very strange, but Mom enjoyed it, and we all attended virtually with her. After the virtual service, we gathered in a circle and prayed for my dad.

"Heavenly Father," my mother began, "we are so very grateful that you brought Robert, my beloved husband, into our lives. We thank you for the many years this wonderful man has blessed our lives." Choking back tears, she couldn't continue.

I finished for her. "Please, Heavenly Father, restore my father to health. Help him conquer this dreaded virus. Give us all the courage we lack to face this uncertain future. Guide and direct our paths. We pray in Jesus' name." Everyone said, "Amen." My mother and I hugged and cried. Katlin joined our hug, and she, too, had tears in her eyes.

Wiping away the tears, my mother proclaimed, "Now it's time for Sunday School." She led an inspiring lesson on the ten lepers Jesus healed.

"If God can heal ten lepers, surely he will heal Grandpa," Katlin surmised.

"Of course he can," Mom told her. "But sometimes God decides it's time for a person to leave this earth and join him in heaven."

"Maybe God needs a doctor there," Oliver offered in his unflappable way.

"Let's hope not just now," Mom replied. It was as close to God as we had all been together in a long time. It felt nice. Warm. I glanced at Nathan. He had not participated directly, but he was watching.

The weather was as good as it gets in St. Louis, and I was eager to get out and meet with friends. Many restaurants had created safe outside dining. I still wasn't ready to dine inside, although it was allowed on a limited basis, but outside seemed fine. Mom was glad to stay with the kids, and to tell the truth, I think they were all glad to see me go. I first wanted to see Grace. She was delighted to get the call. Our first scheduled date had to be canceled because of rain. That's the thing about outdoor dining—it only works in perfect weather. Not too hot. Not too cold. Definitely not in the rain.

When we finally got together, I ran to her...then stopped short. Hugging was not on the virus protocol. We bumped elbows.

"I'm so glad to see you," I cried. "I've missed you so much."

"I've missed you too," Grace told me. "I miss so many people. I miss the gym and I miss my clients. I miss getting paid. Don't you miss work?"

I hadn't thought about work in so long, I took a long breath before answering. "I miss some aspects of work, but honestly, I've been so busy being a mom and housewife, I haven't had much time to miss work. I do miss the people—some of them, anyway. I also miss being really good at something. As a wife and mother, I feel like I fail every day."

I told her the whole gruesome story of how Megan came to the house and all that had transpired since then.

When I finished, Grace blew out a deep breath. "It's amazing that you stayed together at all after that. I suppose I always feared Dan would cause trouble someday. That's why I gave you so much grief over it."

"I know you tried to warn me. But I was in such denial about so many things. How I ignored my kids. How I ignored my marriage. I think my career was all that really mattered. I thought I could do anything without consequences. I'm not even sure who that person was anymore. In a way, I'm glad the whole thing with Megan happened—not the sleeping with Nathan part. That hurt me deeply."

"What's good for the goose…" Grace began.

"It doesn't really work that way, but even with my hurt, I have trouble faulting him. I don't think he cared for Megan at all. He was just mad and somehow thought it would make us even, I guess. But you're right. We're lucky to still be together. I called my staff from Jonas last week. About half are separated or divorced. Kari actually was abused by her husband and ended up in a shelter for a while."

We sat together in silence for moment as what I just said sank in. "On another note," Grace added with a big smile, "I found someone. His name is Ryan Coffman. He was a client, and we started dating before the pandemic. He's a brewmaster at AB. Imagine that. He's so perfect for me. He loves working out, and he's very outdoorsy. We go camping and fishing. We live together now."

"Grace, that's wonderful!" I cried. "I'm so glad for you. What do you think your future holds?"

"Ah," she laughed, "in 2020, who knows what the future holds? We don't even know if we have a future, right? My gym still isn't open, but I'm doing some private training. It's quite lucrative. I'm making almost as much as I was at the gym. I'd love to work with you."

"I'd like that too, but without a job, I don't think I can afford you. I tried to order a treadmill. It was supposed to be my Mother's Day gift, but it still hasn't come. I tried to get weights, but they were sold out. It's crazy the things you can't get. Last week I went to three stores before I found peas. *Peas*, for crying out loud! Every time I go into a store, I know something on my list won't be there. It's just crazy."

"Our generation has never experienced shortages. It's hard for us. Ryan and I tried to order some new furniture for his house, but it takes at least three months to get anything. We gave up and found what we needed on craigslist. At least that still works."

I was feeling on top of the world when I got home. I'd had a lunch—a real lunch with a friend. We had actual in-person conversation. Oh, how I had missed that. But it would not last. I opened the door, took one look at my mother, and instantly knew what had happened. She didn't need to say it. My father, the cornerstone of my life, was gone. We both collapsed on the floor and cried and cried and cried. Katlin joined us. Oliver was very quiet.

And with that devastating news, August 2020 was over. By the end of August, the U.S. had recorded almost 6,000,000 cases of the virus and nearly 176,000 deaths, including Robert Krieger, my dear father. Just when I thought things couldn't get any darker, they did. It seemed that all the light in the world had gone out. I was even angry at the sun for shining.

As if to prove my point, Hurricane Laura, a powerful Category 4 hurricane, made landfall at Cameron Parish in southwestern Louisiana on August 27 with winds up to 150 mph. The storm surge, in excess of fifteen feet, caused heavy damage along the coast and inland to Lake Charles, breaking water systems and severely damaging the electrical grid.

In California, the opposite of water—fire—was creating a disaster in the making. The Walbridge fire, part of the LNU Lightning Complex fires, was spreading. The western wildfires were only getting started.

The Midwest was not to be excluded from the 2020 disasters. On August 10, a rare and powerful derecho with winds up to 100 mph traveled 770 miles from South Dakota to Ohio, causing widespread damage to millions of acres of corn and soybean crops, not to mention damage to homes, businesses, and vehicles.

It seemed like God himself was trying to talk to us. Visons of Revelation danced in my head.

# September 2020 – Darkness Covered the Earth

Somehow, we recovered enough to pick ourselves up from the floor and continue with life. Mom had already called Korie. Nathan called Adam. But we couldn't do much except feel terribly sad, lost, and miserable. Nathan was a gem. He took the kids to a park. I had no idea where. I expect they talked and played while my mother and I cried. We tried to talk about my father, but nothing seemed to come out. It was hard for me to fully understand what she was feeling. I think it was mostly numbness and disbelief. My father was her whole life. I was so glad she was with us when it happened. I couldn't imagine her suffering this loss alone.

My grief was overwhelming. My father was my anchor throughout my life. He was the font of all knowledge. If you wanted to know the best recording of Mozart's *The Magic Flute,* he would know. If you wanted to know the origins of the Blues, he would know. If you wanted to know the history of the Peloponnesian War, ask my father. If you wanted to know what countries border the Black Sea, my father would know off the top of his head without needing to consult a map. He knew everything and everyone loved him, our family most of all. When most of my friends were battling with their father in high school, he was my best friend. When I said I wanted to study Japanese, he calmly asked why and what I would do with it. He never said, "That's a lousy major." Maybe he should have. I'm sure he must have had some disappointment that none of us wanted to be a doctor. If he did, he never expressed it.

He was, of course, pleased that Korie became a nurse, but he never had favorites. If he did, we didn't know. How on earth do you say goodbye to a father like that? I simply couldn't. The only thing he didn't know was how to avoid getting or how to cure this awful virus.

Nathan brought a pizza home for dinner, but I don't remember if I ate any. My mother took a piece and stared at it for a while then excused herself. I suspect she cried herself to sleep. So did I.

The next day, we had to discuss what came next. We were in a global pandemic. Normal funeral arrangements would never be allowed. The church was not holding in-person services, and I was fairly certain they wouldn't hold a funeral service in the church. Even if they would, I wouldn't want to risk exposing anyone to the virus that killed my father. I wasn't even sure we could bury him. I didn't think my mother would be happy with cremation. Most certainly, a post-funeral reception with a hundred or so people, which was our family's custom, would never happen.

After breakfast, I sat with my mother, and together we called the local funeral home in Washington. They were allowed to bury virus victims, but it would probably be a few days before the hospital would release the body. We could not have an open casket even if we wanted to chance a visitation, which was allowed at the funeral home in Washington with restrictions. My mother thought the risk of someone at the visitation or funeral spreading the virus to all our loved ones was too great. I agreed. Korie knew of a family that had spread the virus this way and lost three more members. Surely my father would not want to risk any family members getting the virus for a funeral. Saving people who had the virus was what he had died for, after all.

The next day we called my parents' pastor. He was so kind. Since my parents had already selected a burial plot in the church cemetery, he suggested a small graveside service. It would follow virus protocol with everyone six feet apart, wearing masks and outdoors. There would only be five chairs, set appropriately apart. There would be no hugging or conversing after the service. We would depart, and my dear father would be committed to the ground. All I could think was that the virus took my father from me, and now it was taking my opportunity to grieve him properly. It just kept getting worse and worse.

My mother insisted Adam not come home for the funeral. I knew he really wanted to, but it was dangerous to fly during a pandemic, and there wasn't going to be much of a funeral anyway. I suggested that I could have Grace come and FaceTime with Adam during the funeral so he could feel like he was there. It seemed to be the best solution of our limited options.

Korie presented a different problem. She was a nurse around virus patients every day. Her husband and her kids were staying with her in-laws so she wouldn't risk infecting them if she should get sick. But we couldn't keep any of them away from the service. She needed this to grieve as much as we did. She would wear her most secure protection and stay away from all of us, even her kids. It was all too hard to even contemplate. There were no good solutions. Only one incomprehensible, unacceptable alternative.

My mother spent some time talking to Pastor Hicks. I listened from the kitchen. I was glad she had him to comfort her. She gave him my father's life story—where he was born, where he went to school, and when they were married. As I listened to her reciting the details of his life, it seemed so empty. Those dates and places weren't my dad. He was so much more than that. But now, because he wanted to help during a pandemic, he was gone. What good did it do for him to be so noble? The degrees and service seemed so empty. He was so much more than all those numbers and dates and places. He was my captain, my safe port in every storm. How would I—would we—go on without him? I cried, my whole body shaking with grief and anger and sorrow.

When my mother had finished talking with the pastor, Oliver and Katlin came up to her and asked where Grandpa was. She pulled them close and gave them the most beautiful vision of heaven I had ever heard. She was, after all, a consummate Sunday School teacher. If it would have been a profession, she would have been at the top. She told them how in heaven there was no pain nor sorrow nor hunger. There was only joy at being close to God. In heaven, we can see those who came before us. Grandpa would now be with his dear parents and his brother, who died so long ago. And she added, with joy in her words, "I know as well as I know you are standing here before me that someday, when my time here on earth is done, I will be with him too."

"We don't want you to go to heaven," my children said in unison. I think that might be one of the few things they ever agreed on.

"I don't want to go now either," she said gently. "I want to see you two and your cousins grow into amazing people. But when God calls us home, we must go."

"Just don't answer him," Oliver nearly shouted. "You could say you don't hear. I do that all the time."

"Well, that's not very honest, is it, Oliver?" she asked softly. "There's no fooling God. He knows everything, even when you hide from your parents."

"You better stop that, Oliver," Katlin teased, poking at him. "God is watching you."

"You're mean," he shouted. *Ah,* I thought, *there are the kids I know.*

"Enough," my mother admonished. "Someday, a long, long, long time from now, you two will enter heaven, and I'll be there to greet you."

"I don't think either of us is good enough to get to heaven," Katlin said.

"Well, you have a lot of time to work on it then, but you don't get to heaven by being good. You get to heaven because you believe Jesus died and rose for you. You do both believe in Jesus, don't you?"

Once again in unison, they said, "Of course we do."

"Keep him in your hearts always and try your best to do as he would, and we'll all see Grandpa again someday in heaven."

With that perfect confirmation, Oliver and Katlin ran outside to play. I always knew there was an advantage to having a Sunday School teacher for a mother. She made my heart much lighter too.

I came over and gave her a quick kiss on the cheek. "Thank you, Mom. That was lovely. I think it really helped Katlin and Oliver. I could see the sadness in their eyes lift. You were wonderful."

"And what about you, dear? Did it help you understand?"

"Yes, it did. More than I can say," I said and gave her another quick kiss before retiring to my room, where I wept again. This time I understood it was more for me. I did understand and believe that my father was now in glory in heaven, but it didn't stop me from feeling a terrible emptiness in my heart. I dried my eyes, took up my pen and paper, and wrote my feelings in a poem.

Nathan entered the room shortly after I had finished. "We've ordered Pasta Hut spaghetti for supper. Can you come down?"

"I wrote a poem about my father," I told him, handing over the poem. "What do you think?"

After a few minutes, Nathan replied, "It's beautiful, Roni. You should read it at the funeral."

"I couldn't. I'd just end up sobbing, yet again."

"Then why don't I read it for you?" he offered.

"Yes, please. That would be awesome," I said, giving him a chaste kiss on the cheek. He drew me into a strong hug that warmed my soul. Whatever happened with us in the future, I would always remember that moment and be grateful to Nathan for giving me just what I needed when I needed it most.

The next two days passed in a blur. Nathan's parents sent us a huge ham. It was thoughtful, I think. At least it solved the "what's for dinner?" problem when none of us wanted to cook. We got a huge plant from the staff of the hospital. My mother was touched by that. A few more casseroles and fruit baskets appeared at the door with a flood of cards. My mother carefully read each one and placed them in a keepsake box.

The day of the funeral, if the tiny graveside gathering could be called that, came at last. The funeral home sent a limousine all the way from Washington to collect us. I had braved going inside a department store to get us all appropriate black attire. My mother had accompanied me and selected a simple but sophisticated black suit. She also found a lovely little black hat. I picked out a more stylish black dress with the hope of being able to wear it someplace less sad someday. Even though the store was open, the dressing room was closed, so we had to guess at our sizes. I got a darling navy dress for Katlin and a new dark suit for Oliver. This was his first real suit. It had been so long since I bought Oliver anything but jeans that I wasn't sure what size to get. I bought two sizes. It was the larger one that turned out to be a perfect fit. Nathan was well stocked with dark suits, so he was fully prepared. He hadn't worn a suit in months, and I'm sure it felt a little uncomfortable. None of us had put on anything without an elastic waist in so long, we were all uncomfortable. But that's as it should be. None of us wanted to feel comfortable at this moment.

In just over an hour, the limousine pulled into the cemetery of St. Mark's Church. Korie and her family were already there, her kids running circles around the gravesite. Grace was there too, her tripod in place attached to her phone. Nathan's brother Collin and his girlfriend Stefanie were there too. As a flash of light sparkled from Stefanie's hand, I realized I needed to amend her title to Collin's fiancée. I knew they had moved in together during quarantine, but since Nathan and I hadn't talking all that much, I guess I missed the news. I made a mental note to congratulate them. Aunt Mary and Uncle Stan had come. They stood more than six feet from the rest of us out of an abundance of caution. Several nurses and doctors from the hospital were sprinkled around the site. I gave my mother's hand a little squeeze and softly whispered, "We can do this together, OK?" She smiled back, tears welling in her eyes. This was probably the hardest thing she'd ever had to do.

We walked to the arranged chairs and took our seats. I desperately wanted Korie to sit with us, but she was on the front lines fighting the virus. That made her too risky. Damn, damn, damn that awful virus. Nathan and our kids filled the other chairs. I was so proud of all three of them. They looked like they could be at a state funeral, so somber and well behaved—well, Nathan was always well behaved. The thought made me smile.

Pastor Hicks stepped up to the little podium and began, "Come to me, all you who are weary and burdened, and I will give you rest. Take my yoke upon you and learn from me, for I am gentle and humble in heart, and you will find rest for your souls. For my yoke is easy and my burden is light. These words of Jesus are recorded in Matthew chapter 11. I hope they will give some comfort to you gathered here to remember Robert Krieger. I've known Robert and Helen for nearly 20 years. I can safely say I've known few people more faithful and more full of the Spirit than these two. The apostle Paul tells us in Galatians that 'the fruit of the Spirit is love, joy, peace, forbearance, kindness, goodness, faithfulness, gentleness and self-control.' All those things describe Robert Krieger.

"He was a physician of remarkable skill. His patients listened to him. His coworkers admired him. His family loved him. He had a good life here in Washington. Then last March, a virus that spread rapidly around the world changed everything. Robert didn't have to return to the hospital or fight the virus on the front lines. He was semi-retired, and no one would have criticized him for staying safe. No one but Robert. He was needed and he went. It cost him his life—his life on earth, that is. For Robert is now with his Lord. He has seen his Savior's face and is in full glory. Robert has no more pain or sadness or want. No more patients he can't heal or who won't heed his good advice. No more sickness, no more death. But we here on earth still weep our loss. Don't be shy about mourning Robert. It is a great loss, and it's OK to mourn our loss. Even our Savior wept when he heard his friend Lazarus had died. We will miss you, Robert. Now Robert's son-in-law Nathan would like to read a poem written by his wife, Roni."

Nathan cautiously stepped to the podium and read:

**"My Father" by Veronica Krieger Wright**

*My father was much more*
*Than just the days of his life.*
*More than dates and places and degrees,*
*More than years of service and honors received.*
*He was the loving captain of my life.*
*He led my ship in stormy waters,*
*He guided me to find calm seas.*

*My father was my cornerstone,*
*He built my life's foundation.*
*He set my course on solid ground,*
*And when I stumbled or flew too high, he righted me.*
*He was the source of my inspiration*
*And the fire behind my ambition;*
*He was my guide for all life's journey.*

*Without my father, I'm sinking.*
*He's left a void too deep,*
*An emptiness fills my aching heart*
*With silent screams.*
*My tears flood my world with loss and loneliness.*
*Goodbye, dear father, my friend, my guide,*
*Until we meet again beyond the sky.*

Nathan quietly took his seat.

Then I saw some movement in the bushes behind where Nathan had stood. A man and a woman came out with a guitar. They stood in the pastor's place and sang "It is Well With My Soul." Now nothing could stop the floodgate of tears from opening. Katlin reached over and handed me a tissue. I held her tightly then hugged my mother. The pastor prayed for us, and we all said the Lord's Prayer. Then the pastor sprinkled dirt on the coffin and said, "Ashes to ashes." Whatever else he said was lost to me. It was finished. But our mourning would continue for a long time.

A few people came by, stood six feet away, and offered condolences. Then just like that, it was all over. My father would shortly be lowered into the ground. It was time for us to go home. There would be no funeral feast, no gathering, no hugging the other mourners. All we could do was go home and grieve together in our little family.

As we were getting into the car, my mother asked if we could stop at her neighbor's. The driver agreed. We all got out. As we approached the door, it opened and her sweet dog Daisy sprinted out, wagging her tail wildly and running from my mother to Katlin to Oliver and back again. Mom looked at me. "Can we take her home?" she asked. Immediately there was a chorus of "Please, Mom, please!" from my kids. I looked at Nathan, who was never really a dog person. "Sure," he said. Just like that, we had a dog. By the time we reached our house an hour later, Daisy had shed some of herself on all our new clothes, but the smiles on my kids' face made it all OK, sort of.

My mother was a welcome addition to our family. I couldn't imagine her living in her house in Washington alone, grieving during a pandemic. The kids enjoyed having her here. I enjoyed having her here. Even Nathan, I think, enjoyed having her here. I was learning so much from her, mostly about cooking. As she cooked, I wrote down recipes that had never been recorded. They would now be a part of our family forever. Nathan and I were forced to share a bedroom again. Although it had not advanced to the level of intimacy I was hoping for, we were gradually growing closer. Whatever the cost, seeing Mom smile, even occasionally, made it all worthwhile.

Without my salary, we were struggling financially. Mom knew this and asked to have a private conversation with Nathan and me one evening. "I'd like to pay rent for my stay," she told us.

"Mom, we're delighted to have you here, all of us," I said, looking at Nathan, who was nodding. "It's a lovely offer, but we'll be fine."

"I'm so glad you like having me here because I've decided to rent out my house. The hospital has asked if they could rent it for a doctor who came to replace your father. He's only expected to stay as long as the virus has pressed the hospital to capacity. Once it's over, he'll probably move back to wherever he came from. I think it's a good plan for now, but I don't need the money. Our house is paid for, and I have your father's pension. I'd like you to have the rent money to help with your bills."

"Helen, we really don't—" Nathan began.

"I insist," Mom said with more finality than I had ever heard from her. The discussion was over, as was this month's financial crisis. We were saved, once again. I had to admit that my prayers had been answered with alarming frequency. Maybe God was listening to me. Perhaps it was time for me to come back to regular church attendance, or at least regular virtual attendance.

Now that this was behind us, it was time to think about school. This time last year, my kids had been in school for two weeks. I had been ignoring everything that didn't relate to my father's passing. I opened the emails from the Willow Glen School Board. Due to the ongoing pandemic, our kids' school was not opening school to "in-person learning." That's another new term we got from the pandemic. Of course, kids always learned "in person." We never knew there was an alternative. The pandemic changed that. For the foreseeable future, our kids would be placed on a rotating schedule of "virtual school." Apparently, that meant school on Zoom. Before the pandemic, I had only used Zoom a couple of times. Now my kids would be learning daily from their tablets somewhere in our already crowded house. It made me more grateful than ever for this big house. But where to hold classes was the issue. I held a meeting with my family to discuss the options. Oliver was thrilled that he wasn't going off to first grade. Much to my surprise,

Katlin was rather nonplussed about learning from home. I was sure she would be disappointed not to be going to school. *Note to self: figure out what that's about.*

We all agreed that this schoolwork would never be done properly in their rooms, so we had to come up with desks in other places for each. We also agreed that Katlin and Oliver would not work well in the same room. Our plan was to put Katlin in the living room where Nathan had first tried to put his office. Oliver would be at the dining room table where I could keep a watchful eye on him. He pulled the most menacing face at this suggestion, but I knew it was the only solution, at least for now. My mother sat quietly during most of the discussion but found her voice near the end.

"I think it might be very fortunate that I've decided to stay. I did teach elementary school for 25 years," she reminded us. "Mostly fifth grade, but I think I could be a big help."

"Wow, I nearly forgot. If you don't mind helping, that would be marvelous," I said.

"I think God put me here for a reason. This must be it."

"Hurray, Teacher Grandma!" both kids shouted.

"Can we still call you Grandma while you're teaching?" Katlin asked.

"I think that would be lovely," she replied. I smiled. After my dismal effort at home schooling last spring, this was going to be a piece of cake, I thought. But nothing is ever quite that simple.

Our first week of Zoom school was an absolute disaster. Just about everything went wrong. We missed several classes because our Zoom wasn't connecting or I misread the time or simply couldn't make Oliver sit at the table. Oliver kept disappearing under the dining room table. I didn't think they were learning anything other than how to fight, not just with me, but with my sweet mother. On top of that, they were locked in the house all day with nothing to do between classes but bicker and annoy everyone else, including Nathan. I decided there must be a better way.

I started searching the internet for virtual school discussion groups. I discovered a mom group that talked about creating small "learning pods." A learning pod was a group of families from the same school and neighborhood with like minds on pandemic safety who would meet in their homes and follow the Zoom classes together. This must be the solution. I asked Oliver and Katlin for names of classmates in our neighborhood. They came up with ten names.

I've never been active in my neighborhood, or in anything other than work, so I didn't know these people well. I asked the school for contact information and was (reluctantly) given some phone numbers. I immediately started calling. My criteria for our pod were families with kids Katlin and/or Oliver's age who worked from home and had little exposure to other people, meaning the virus. I found five families that fit my criteria. We agreed to meet at our house, outside to reduce our exposure and with masks on, which made refreshments difficult. Every family had the same issues we faced. They all wanted to find a group their children could study with but were also concerned about exposure to the virus.

We agreed to set guidelines. None of the families went to work in a situation where they were exposed to lots of other people. Everyone agreed to limit their exposure to family members who were following virus protocol, no indoor dining or gatherings, and only essential shopping. Our kids would meet outdoors if at all possible and stay close to six feet apart whenever they could. Our children would learn together three days a week and "do school" the other two days from home. The only thing left to decide was who would supervise the learning. My mother suddenly spoke up.

"Hi, I'm Roni's mom, and I'm living with them. I'm a retired elementary schoolteacher, and I would be delighted to be their teacher."

Problem solved. Our pod was now created. One family backed out. They thought it was still too risky, too much exposure to other people and possibly the virus. So that left four families. Three third graders (two girls and one boy), three first graders (two boys and one girl), and two kindergarten students. Each family would make space in their garage or on their back porch for studying. The kids would have lunch together, spread out, and playtime between lessons. I liked these people. They all had lives similar to ours. One or both of the parents were forced to work from home because of the pandemic, and they all felt like failures with "virtual learning." We shared a glass of wine. They were all wine and beer drinkers—more in their favor—and they all cared deeply about their children. I thought this would be the beginning of some great friendships. This time I wasn't wrong.

Since we had agreed to keep classes outside as much as possible, as the virus spreads more easily inside, we now needed to upgrade our patio. First, we needed to replace the aging table where the children would work. Our table was a little wobbly and not at all appropriate for children. That was fairly easy, but like everything during a pandemic, it was back-ordered. Not too bad. It would probably come in a month. Then we decided we needed an outdoor heater so the children could keep studying outside as the weather turned colder. That was more problematic. We weren't the only family with this idea. The heaters were back-ordered two to three months. We placed our order, keeping fingers crossed that this year we would see a long, warm fall. In this, at least, luck was with us. Classes started, and the children were actually learning together for the first time since the pandemic began. *Thank you, God, for one small miracle.*

Finally, the long, long month of September came to a close. The month began with my father's funeral, but it ended with my mother comfortably ensconced in our home and teaching once again. Nathan and I were sharing a bedroom. My children were learning with other children, and I felt for the first time in a very long time that maybe, just maybe, we would survive this pandemic. But the news wasn't all good.

By the end of September, more than 7,000,000 people in the U.S. had contracted the virus. There were 31,000 people hospitalized, and almost 200,000 people had died.

Hurricane Sally made landfall in Gulf Shores, Alabama, with wind gusts up to 100 mph. It was a slow-moving storm bringing heavy rain to multiple states and causing flooding in Florida and Alabama. In mid-September, five storms churned around the Atlantic Ocean simultaneously for only the second time on record. September 18 marked the second time on record that three named storms (Wilfred, Alpha, and Beta—they had run out of English names) all formed on the same day. The only other time this was known to happen was August 1893.

Meanwhile, on the West Coast, wildfires were burning from California to Washington. California nearly doubled its annual record with over 4.1 million acres burned. Oregon also had historic levels of wildfire damage with over 2,000 structures burned. Wildfires destroyed several small towns in California, Oregon, and Washington. A massive cloud of yellow-brown smoke from the fires blanketed the West Coast. The dense smoke produced hazardous air quality for weeks. Citizens were warned to stay indoors. Anyone who thought they might escape the virus outdoors were struck with the dangerous wildfire fog.

The new normal included wearing a mask, staying six feet apart, washing hands, and mostly staying home. All activities with more than ten people were discouraged. Restaurants were mostly closed to indoor dining. Churches and other venues were virtual or limited to 25 percent capacity. Travel was nearly impossible.

Almost anything you wanted to buy was hard to find. Consumers were buying online in record numbers, creating mounds of packaging waste. Many restaurants offered contactless take-out. Services without contact were popular. Our new church even offered drive-up communion. We were finding ways to survive.

# October 2020 – Indian Summer

October started well. The weather was mild, and the kids were learning in their "pod" outside. They were getting along well, and all seemed fine. The weather in St. Louis is *always* an issue. October can be insufferably hot or bitter cold, with torrents of rain or dry as a desert. You never know. So, with everything that had happened in 2020, a mild October seemed like a gift. A part of me wanted to think about how the upcoming holidays would happen during a pandemic, but I also wanted to take one day at time.

We were all still reeling from my father's death and had moments of great sadness, but our Sunday virtual sermons were helping. This church spoke of love and forgiveness. In last week's sermon, Pastor Morley talked about conflict. He said, "Living as a family means we have to contend with each other. We are all imperfect people, and sometimes we just might annoy each other." I think we all laughed at that.

He said we should use our conflict to grow. Then he added, "We all fall short of perfection in life, but God will never stop loving us. If you ever doubt, remember how God used so many imperfect people in the Bible to tell his story. Adulterers, prostitutes, thieves—all have a place in his kingdom. You do too." I felt a few tears fall from my eyes as I looked at Nathan. His eyes were gleaming too.

We fell short, but we still believed in redemption. It felt so good to know God loves us with all our failings and blemishes. It was helping Nathan and me to heal. Not completely. Such a severe wound wouldn't heal easily. We both knew that, but thanks to the virus, we were stuck not only with being in the same house, but in the same bedroom. In our prepandemic life, one of us, probably Nathan, would have left, and healing would have been impossible. Without my mother in the house, Nathan would have stayed in the maid's room, making healing more difficult. Without my mother encouraging us to attend virtual church with her, we would have forgotten about forgiveness. Seeing each other each night made our desire for reconciliation grow. I felt him getting closer, not physically, but emotionally. I knew it wouldn't be long before something would happen. We just needed a little more faith. Our weekly virtual services were melting the chill, little by little. One can't hear God's words of forgiveness over and over without it sinking in somewhere.

By the middle of October, my mother had hit a snag in her lessons. Katlin's class was supposed to study life in Germany, Austria, and Switzerland. Since Mom was so familiar with those countries, she did not agree with what they were learning. She shared her concerns with me, and I agreed. I called the teacher.

I forgot what a terrible time this was for the poor teachers. They not only had to prepare lessons, but they had to navigate a new technology for them and their students. The issues they faced were mountainous. Once they figured out how to teach a lesson on Zoom, they had to deal with vastly unequal student technology. No two students had the same technology. Some had PC computers and some had Apple. Some had all the hardware and internet access available, while others had neither equipment nor internet access. Some had parents who understood the technology and taught their students seamlessly, and some had parents who didn't understand it at all and failed over and over again to connect. Some parents just did the lessons for their kids, and some kids, like Oliver, spent half of each lesson under the desk or absent. Most parents were trying their best to supervise their kids while working from home and managing their own Zoom meetings. Learning was hit or miss at best.

All this during a pandemic. Teachers were concerned that just coming to school to teach a virtual lesson could put them and their families at risk of getting the virus. It was an impossible situation, as was my conversation with Katlin's teacher, Ms. Andrews. She threw up her hands and said, "If you think you can do better, be my guest. Create a virtual lesson for third graders about a foreign country and teach it so they understand on Zoom. You're welcome to try and do better. I'm exhausted. I can barely manage these lessons in reading, math, and science. Anything else is just too much."

That should have been the end of the discussion, but I saw it as a challenge. The one thing I knew and knew well was the history and geography of Europe. I had been to all these places many times. I had mapped out tours, selected the most historic sites, lectured on history, and I spoke the language—well, at least German. I marched into my office and started pulling down my old travel guides. Before long, two hours had passed in which I had amassed volumes of pertinent information and photographs. I began serious work on a course on central Europe. Challenge accepted.

I spent hours digging through my files and photos, pulling out the countless materials I had collected over the years. I found all the files on Germany, Austria, and Switzerland then separated them into geography, history, and culture. I had decided I would concentrate on those three areas. The idea was to give them a flavor of what these countries were like. I found descriptions of the fertile Rhine River valleys dotted with ancient castles and vineyards. I copied my description of the picturesque villages in Switzerland with their majestic mountains topped with a gentle layer of pure white snow. I found a description of cutting a Christmas tree on the Swiss mountainside and sledding down the mountain with the tree in tow.

Of course, I had to navigate the history carefully. I wasn't about to dissect WWII and the Nazi movement for elementary students. How could I possibly explain the horrors of concentration camps or their

121

effort to exterminate an entire race of people? I wrote about the ancient Germanic tribes and how they created a unified country while the Austrian empire was collapsing. I knew I had to address WWII, but delicately. Using a history book I had bought in Germany, I carefully and factually tackled the basics of that history.

Geography was also challenging. I decided to make several maps to show how boundaries changed over the years. Here I hit a roadblock. None of the maps I found were simple enough for elementary students. I knew what I wanted them to look like but not how to draw them. Fortunately, I lived with an architect who just happened to love maps. Nathan was drawing maps when he was Katlin's age. I knew he couldn't resist helping. I carefully presented my problem to Nathan.

"I see your problem. I don't think I could find maps that would show today's boundaries and the boundaries of, say, 1900 in a format easy for elementary students to understand," Nathan said.

"But you could draw a map, couldn't you? It doesn't need a lot of detail. Some cities, rivers, and mountain ranges would work."

"You know I've always loved maps. I think you're trying to tempt me with my passion for mapmaking," he said smiling.

"Just think of all the young minds you could influence with your clever maps," I teased.

"You are sly. Of course I'll do it. Not for all those young minds, but for Katlin. I'll even get her to help me. I've always wanted to find a way to pass on my love of maps to my kids. This will be fun. Thanks for asking." He leaned over and gave me a little kiss. At first it took me by surprise. Then I reached up and kissed him on the mouth with a passion I thought we had lost. Clearly, it wasn't lost, just hiding. That evening, after the kids went to bed, we made up. Really exhilaratingly, energetically made up. Not everything was resolved in a few minutes of passion, but it was the biggest step we had taken this year.

As I lay there in bed, exhausted, sleepy, happier than I can remember being, I started to wonder how long it had been since we'd felt like this.

In love, in like, happy with the marriage. I thought back to New Year's in that great hotel room at the Chase. I thought everything was so good, but was it? How could I have betrayed my marriage vows if everything was great? How could Nathan? Maybe everything hadn't been great for a long time. Maybe I'd been pushing something under the surface. I could see what workaholics we had both become. We had been so blinded by our desire to excel in our careers, we forgot who we were, who we wanted to be. We forgot this beautiful family we had created. We forgot to take care of each other. We'd had a lot of time in the past year to take a new look at ourselves. I didn't much like what I'd seen of the old me. Perhaps a new me could emerge from this lost year. A better me. A more present me in every sense of the word. I vowed at that moment to keep searching for that person I could be. Not just a better me, but a better us.

With my history research of Germany, Austria, and Switzerland completed, I presented it over Zoom to Ms. Andrew. She was beyond impressed.

"Wow, Roni, I don't think I've ever seen a modern history lesson on this region so well presented. You cover almost every aspect of their history, geography, and culture so succinctly. All perfectly positioned for elementary students. And these maps…they're amazing. Where did you find them?"

"My husband made the maps. He's an architect but also an amateur mapmaker. I couldn't find anything that covered this modern area well. He really enjoyed doing this."

"Well, I have to say, this is just wonderful from top to bottom. Do you mind if I share it with other classes? I'm sure all the teachers would like to use it. I may even show it at the district level."

When our meeting was over, I was feeling better about myself than I had in about nine months. This feeling was much deeper than the self-confidence I had in my hospitality career. This filled my soul.

My mother introduced my presentation of Germany, Austria, and Switzerland to her students the next day. I watched as she led them through the PowerPoint presentation I had prepared. They were all fully engaged. I made notes of their reactions, the things that piqued their interest, and areas that were less engaging. I made some corrections. I wanted to expand this work. I ran back to my office and put the presentation into booklet form. Then I started a booklet for elementary students on Japan since I knew a lot about that country too.

With October winding down, the holidays were fast approaching. New guidelines for trick-or-treating presented a whole new challenge. No more handing goodies to costumed princesses and ghouls. No more said costumed children sticking germ-laced hands into a bowl of said goodies. All activities must be at a distance—six feet, at least. All treats must be individually packaged so a trick-or-treater can grab one bag, carefully placed without touching anything or anyone else. Of course, masks were not only a part of the costume, but necessary pandemic attire. Nathan was a Halloween fanatic. He loved everything about the holiday and was determined to find a way to make it fun. We decorated our front yard with signs and ghosts. He even got a costume for Daisy. He created a clothesline of sorts across the yard from which we hung bags of prepackaged treats. We kept our distance, but few children came. Most parents just kept their kiddos home.

It would have been a sad Halloween but for our carefully chosen pod. Since our children were studying with a group of children all from families with little virus exposure, we agreed this was a relatively safe group to party with—outdoors, of course. Our pod arranged a progressive Halloween party with different courses and activities at each house. We had dessert, which I had become quite good at making. I found some amazing spider cookies online and had a great deal of fun making them with my children. I also made some cupcakes for the kids to decorate themselves. All were served with plenty of wine, beer, and apple juice. We were blessed with a beautiful evening, and the party went off perfectly. Once we got over what we couldn't do, we found something every bit as good. Maybe better. But I knew Thanksgiving and Christmas would not be as easy. And nothing like any other year. More challenges were ahead.

By the end of October, there were 9,000,000 confirmed cases of the virus in the U.S., and 47,000 people were currently hospitalized. The death toll from the virus had reached more than 222,000. That was only those who died from catching the virus. The consequences of the closures and life changes from the pandemic were far greater, as we would learn shortly.

The pandemic was not the only event ravaging our world. On October 14, Colorado's Cameron Peak Fire surged to become the largest in state history, burning more than 208,000 acres, surpassing the record set less than two months before.

If there was hopeful news to be found in the pandemic, it was that at least two American companies, Pfizer and Moderna, were rapidly developing a vaccine that would protect us from the virus. The trials were reportedly going well, and they hoped to receive Emergency Use Authorization from the FDA by the end of the year. It seemed too good to be true. But hope was alive.

# November 2020 – The Storm Rages On

We had settled into a new normal, or so we thought. We were adjusting to all the pandemic rules. Any time we were outside, we wore a face mask. We had a massive collection of masks by now—some homemade, some from the store, and a couple designer ones, just for show. I even had a shirt with a large collar that pulled up and attached to my ears, creating a mask. There was no going out to restaurants, of course, or just about anywhere else. Most of our favorite entertainment— movie theaters, museums, the Science Center—were either closed or had limited access. Even if some attractions were open, we only went to outdoor activities. But we were managing the curbside ordering process as best we could. Delivery was available from almost every restaurant, from fast food to fancy. My cooking was improving daily. We kept six feet apart in the park or grocery store or anywhere we went, which wasn't many places. The children were learning together, with my mother at the helm in our safe pod. Nathan, who had never stopped working for a minute—always from home, of course—was locked in his office working constantly.

I had found a new purpose. I had revised my first lesson and nearly finished the lesson on Japan. I was hard at work on three others. I now called the booklets "Connection with Our World." The district had agreed to add the first lesson to their curriculum. The bigger news was that one of the district directors had sent my first lesson to a scholastic book publisher. I didn't have a response yet, but I was hopeful.

Actually, I was as hopeful as a person in the middle of a pandemic could be. My marriage was on the mend, my children were learning, and I was becoming closer to them than I'd ever been. My mother was navigating her way through her grief, as were we all. We all knew that the upcoming holidays would be different in nearly every way. Travel was still very risky. Visiting family was still risky. It had been almost a year since we last saw Nathan's family, and I suspected it would be much longer. I was just contemplating what our holidays might look like when Nathan entered the room, a look of horror on his face.

"What's happened? You look like you just lost a dear friend."

"I did," he replied, trying hard to hold back tears. "It's my cousin Ralph. He was found dead yesterday in his restaurant. He hanged himself. It's so horrible. My uncle could hardly get the words out." With that, he melted down.

I raced to his side and held him in my arms while he sobbed. Ralph had opened his dream restaurant six months before the pandemic hit and the quarantine closed everything. We knew he had fallen deeply into debt to open the restaurant, but the opening went well. We visited the restaurant last November when we were in the Chicago area. I could easily see why it had cost so much. The decor was spectacular. He had artifacts from around the world, which was the restaurant's theme. He offered specialties from every corner of the globe. It was an exciting idea, and I think he would have done very wel—except for the global pandemic that closed his restaurant as the debt mounted.

"Oh, Nathan, I'm so sorry. What can we do?"

"Nothing, just nothing. I feel so helpless. I knew the restaurant was in serious trouble, as many are. It wasn't set up for carryout. It was the kind of place you went for an elegant evening. I guess he couldn't face this final failure."

"But didn't Ralph have a fiancée and a baby on the way? Surely he didn't want to leave them?" I said the wrong thing. Nathan's tears were flowing harder than ever.

"I talked to him about a month ago. He was so excited about being a father. He didn't want his son to see him as a failure. We all told him no one could've predicted what's happened in 2020. But he wouldn't listen. I suppose he thought his options were exhausted. I would have liked to have gone to see him when I knew he was struggling, but it was too risky. Before the pandemic, we would have gone to see a concert or gone on a road trip to help with the despair, but what could we have done now? We're not traveling. We're not staying in hotels. I just feel so impotent."

"Well, we know you're not that," I said, trying to lighten the mood. He gave me a "not now" look, and I quickly retreated to a more somber position. "You were a good friend to Ralph. We both know that. You would have done something, anything, if you'd known how bad this was." There was so little I could say. I did understand how he felt. I, too, knew the pain of suicide. It was a college friend, years ago. Suicide leaves behind a massive void. Loved ones are left with so many questions that can never be answered.

"I can't even go to the funeral, if there even is one," Nathan sobbed. "I can't travel to Chicago. It's just too damn risky."

"We could send a plant to your aunt and uncle," I offered.

"Oh, yeah. A plant. Sorry your son's dead. Here's a plant. Hope you don't kill it."

In every successful relationship, one person needs to know when to stop talking. I had hit the wall. I had nothing more to say that would make any difference to Nathan. The only thing he needed to hear now was, "I'm so terribly sorry, Nathan. This is just awful. Please let me know what I can do."

"If I figure it out, I'll let you know," he said. "For now, I think I need to be alone. I'm going for a walk. But first, I need to call my brother. Oh, God. That will be hard."

"Maybe you could take your phone to Queeny Park and find a nice bench in the woods. Call your brother from there. It will be just you two and nature."

"That's an excellent idea," he said, smiling through his tears. "I'm glad I married you after all." Then he left, leaving me with an empty feeling. Ralph wasn't my cousin, but I knew him and liked him, very much. It felt so odd with Nathan out of the house. We'd been together in the same house for months. So odd. For a couple who had spent so much of our married lives apart, it now seemed lonelier than I could have ever imagined. It was time to have a little chat with God. It wouldn't change anything, but I knew it would make me feel better. Then I had a chat with my mother too. By the time Nathan returned, we were both feeling slightly better.

They held a simple funeral, but no one came from out of town. Creditors took over Ralph's restaurant. His fiancée left town right after the funeral. She was going back to Canada to be with her parents. She was Canadian, so she was allowed in. Ralph's parents wouldn't be able to go to Canada to see the baby because the Canadian border was closed to non-Canadians. It felt like Ralph was erased everywhere but in our hearts. But he would live there for a long time. The day of the funeral, Nathan and I took advantage of a lovely fall evening and sat outside. We drank a bottle of wine and shared memories of his cousin. He, of course, had many more than me, but I had enough to participate. It wasn't quite the closure that a funeral gives, but it helped.

A week later, I got the most amazing note from the scholastic publishing company reviewing my first little book. They were interested! Not only in my first book, but in a series that would take students around the globe. We scheduled a time to talk (on Zoom, of course) in a couple of weeks. I was thrilled beyond measure. I wasn't quite ready to share this good news with the world, in case it didn't materialize. But I bought a bottle of champagne and shared it with Nathan, my cocreator, later that evening in our room. It led to another delightful evening.

❧

"Mom, are we going to Chicago for Thanksgiving again this year?" Katlin asked the next morning at breakfast. "It was so much fun staying at Grandma Wright's house and going to their country club."

I was actually surprised that Katlin remembered that trip as fun. It had only seemed like work to me. Maybe I was so fixated on the children's behavior that I missed something. But then, I missed a lot last year.

"No, sweetheart. We won't be going to Chicago. It's too risky to travel with the nasty virus out there. We'll just have Thanksgiving here."

"But you don't know how to make a turkey or sweet potatoes or pie!" she shrieked.

"I'll have Grandma Krieger to help. I'd hoped you would've noticed that I'm much better at cooking now."

"Yeah," Oliver piped in, "I told our pod that the virus made you cook."

I smiled in spite of the sting. "I think you're right, Oliver. It did make me learn to cook."

"Well, at least we'll have our cousins Henry and James over for Thanksgiving, won't we?" Katlin asked.

Thankfully, my mother fielded this tough one. "Unfortunately, we can't have them over either. Aunt Korie is a nurse. She takes care of virus patients every day, and that puts them all in a high-risk group. We'll have to have a simple family Thanksgiving with just us in this house."

"That stinks!" shouted Katlin. "Not much of a Thanksgiving!"

"Katlin, that's very rude. Think how lucky we are. We have a grandma who lives with us and can be here for Thanksgiving. Many children won't even have one grandparent at their table. But we can Zoom with Grandma and Grandpa Wright and your cousins."

"Whatever," was Katlin's too-snarky reply.

I let that slip. This was all hard. "I tell you what, each person in the family can pick one dish they want to have for Thanksgiving. Our meal will be turkey with all our picks."

"That sounds like fun," Oliver said.

"Whatever," Katlin said. Clearly it was time to have a chat with Katlin.

Before she went to sleep that night, I went to have a little talk with her. Sitting on the side of her bed, I said, "You were rather snarky with me today. Is there something you want to talk about?" We sat in silence for a few minutes while Katlin was deciding what she wanted to say. Some instinct told me this was a time to be quiet and wait until she was ready to talk.

"You see," she began hesitantly, "there's these girls in my school that are so cool. They were so impressed with our Thanksgiving last year at the country club in Chicago. It made me a little cooler. I wanted to be their friend, but it seemed I was never good enough no matter how hard I tried. I thought it might be fun to text them about another trip to Chicago. That's pretty dumb, isn't it?"

I took a deep breath and prayed that I would say the right thing. "Outside of the fact that these girls are cool, do you really like them?" I asked.

"Well, I guess not."

"It seems to me they were pretty mean to you."

"Yeah, they were. But that's just because I was such a dork."

Another deep breath. "Katlin, there's never an excuse to be mean. Mean is just mean. Are the girls in our pod mean?"

"Oh no, they're really nice, even when I wear that big stupid sweater that's so warm. They never say anything about what I wear or what we do."

"Wouldn't you rather be friends with someone who makes you feel good than someone who makes you feel bad?"

"Yeah, but it's fun to be cool."

"Fun enough to be ridiculed by what you wear?"

"No, I guess not."

"Katlin, I think you've found some true friends this year. It's time to stop worrying about what those mean girls think. You are very cool to me."

"Oh, Mom. Everybody's cool to their mom." She giggled. I do love that giggle.

"If anybody ever tells you again that you're not cool, come to me and I'll put you straight." She smiled as I gave her a hug and kiss. This was the best talk we had ever had. I need to make a point of doing this more often.

The Thanksgiving menu came together quickly. Katlin picked sweet potatoes with marshmallows. I had no idea how to do that, but I was sure Martha Stewart would. Oliver picked chocolate pie. Not a Thanksgiving tradition, but this Thanksgiving was breaking all the traditions anyway. Nathan picked corn. *Corn? Really?* He's such a nerd. Lovable nerd, but nerd no less. My mom picked cranberries, and I picked mashed potatoes because we had to have that anyway. My mother had the kids make Thanksgiving decorations and I bought a bunch more. This was my first time "hosting" Thanksgiving. It was one more 2020 challenge. I wanted to make this meal extra special. I watched tons of videos on everything on the menu except the corn. That was coming from a can. I knew my mother could do this in her sleep, but this was my time to step up. I've always loved a challenge, and I was determined to meet this one head-on.

When the day came, we had a Zoom call with Nathan's family. They all seemed well. His parents had ordered a dinner to be delivered by Uber. His brother was celebrating with his girlfriend, now fiancée. It all felt somber, but we at least had the chance to catch up. Katlin asked if she could be a flower girl. Stefanie was caught without an answer. She recovered well and said, "I'm not sure we'll even have a real wedding.

Those aren't allowed during the pandemic, but I promise, if we do, Katlin will be flower girl and Oliver will be ring bearer." That brought a flood of fun speculation from each. Our Zoom with Korie and her family didn't go quite as well. She had to work and could only talk a short time. Her mother-in-law was in charge of the meal and was only making a turkey breast with store-made sides. I guess she wasn't a cook either. The boys were clearly restless and missing their cousins. It was a bit sad.

My mother set the table with all our lovely decorations. We had turkeys made from paper, ceramics, paper plates, and even chocolate. I was puzzled by the place settings. There was one extra with a large paper chrysanthemum on the chair.

"Isn't there an extra chair?" I asked my mother.

"This one," she answered, pointing to the chrysanthemum chair, "is for your father." That nearly took the breath from me. "Of course," I answered and retreated quickly to the kitchen.

As we sat down with the feast before us, I quickly announced, "Before we all dig into this meal, I think we need to start a new tradition. I'd like each of us to say something we are thankful for. When we've all spoken, we'll say a prayer together. And," I added, "it must be more than just family."

My mother was quick to pick up the challenge. "I'm so very thankful to have my lovely room here in your house. I'm grateful to be teaching again, especially my darling grandchildren. This year has brought more sadness than I've ever known, but you all have made it bearable. Thank you." I quickly jumped up and gave her a hug.

"The next chair," I told them, "is empty because it's where Grandpa would have sat. Grandma placed it there so he could be remembered and, in some way, be part of our feast."

Before that sad note had a chance to spread, Nathan picked up the pace. "I'm thankful," he began, "for this massive house. I always thought it was way too much for us. Maybe God led us to this place because he knew we'd need extra space for a global pandemic." That brought smiles all around. *Yes, Nathan, that was an excellent call. He is a treasure.*

"I'm glad that we have a great backyard where our pod can have recess," Oliver contributed. "If we can't go anyplace, at least we have our yard. And I'm glad for Daisy." Daisy barked her approval. I had awarded her a special dog treat for Thanksgiving.

"I'm glad for our pod," Katlin said. "I'm glad we don't have any of the cool girls from school in the pod. Even if they're not popular, I like the girls in our pod." She gave me a huge smile, and my heart melted. I was so proud, I was floating.

"Roni," Nathan said, pulling me back down to earth. "It's your turn."

Bringing my thoughts back to the table, I had to think quickly. We needed something light. "I'm thankful for Martha Stewart," I said. "Without her, this meal would have been a disaster." That brought laughs all around and set a lively tone for the meal, which was very good. Maybe the turkey was a little dry. I'll have to work on that.

Just as quickly as it arrived, November was over. The U.S. death toll from the virus now stood at 260,000. There were over 13,000,000 confirmed cases. The 96,000 hospitalized patients were straining our hospitals' resources. Too many people ignored the warnings from the CDC and traveled over the Thanksgiving holiday, causing a spike in cases and hospitalizations. Guidelines for managing the virus were as diverse as our country. Some states required masks everywhere. Some only inside. Some didn't require masks at all. Some thought wearing a mask was a political statement, although it seemed to me that the virus attacked all political parties.

A presidential election had been held in November, but for the first time in our nation's long history, the sitting president refused to accept the election results and concede to his opponent. He claimed election fraud and pronounced the election had been stolen, even though state and federal judges (some appointed by said president) dismissed more than fifty lawsuits presented by the president and his allies challenging the election. Political and social unrest never seemed more divisive. Not since the Civil War had our nation been so divided. I truly feared that when January came, the president would still refuse to leave the White House. No one knew exactly what would happen.

A vaccine was rapidly being developed, but the government was spending so much time trying to overturn the election, nobody was preparing for the possibility of mass vaccinations.

Nature was not to be ignored. Tropical Storm Eta was the first tropical storm to make a November landfall in Florida since 1998. Eta was only the twelfth named tropical system to strike the continental U.S. in a single season since records had been kept. Prior to 2020, the season with the most landfalls was 1916, which had nine. 2020 would not be outdone by anyone or anything.

# December 2020 –
# Some Hope, Some Pain,
# Some Holiday

After our subdued and quiet Thanksgiving, we all knew Christmas would be much of the same. No grand parties. No rush through the mall. No visit with Santa. The only thing we could do was decorate, and decorate we did. As soon as Thanksgiving was past, Nathan and I scoured the stores and the Web for every decoration we could find. We weren't the only ones either. Judging by our neighborhood, every family was trying to out decorate the other. Some families on our street who had never decorated before strung up lights and put out all sorts of holiday cheer. One could spot Snoopy, the Grinch, and assorted holiday-decorated animals throughout the neighborhood. I even saw a lighted Christmas-dressed dog opening a mailbox to send a letter to Santa. Leaning into our newfound faith, we found a lively lighted nativity with two bigger-than-life angels. It was surrounded by well-lit trees and lights everywhere. We were determined a global pandemic would not stop Christmas. At least not in our yard.

December continued the mild pattern we had seen all fall, but even a mild St. Louis December was too cold for outdoor classes. Our pod of children had to find a new place to study. The pod parents all agreed that a space at least open to outside was safest from the virus. So, we set up "school" in our garages. Fortunately, the outdoor heater Nathan and I had ordered more than three months ago arrived in time for the colder weather. My mother armed herself with long underwear, hats, scarves, and mittens to protect herself from the cold and carried on with class. My kids liked to say they had Nordic blood and didn't feel the cold. In any case, our pod with virtual school was soldiering on.

Nathan continued to work from his home office. We hardly ever saw him during the day. With no out-of-town trips or luncheons, he was getting more done than ever before. His office was cluttered with plans spread everywhere, but he had his system and was growing more comfortable with working from home. As his company had no plans for going back to the office, that was a good thing.

I had another meeting with the scholastic book company. It was, of course, virtual. No one met anyone in person these days. On the call were five members of the book company team and our school district director who first brought my book to their attention. I had worked all week on my presentation, and I was prepared for their first question.

"Tell us, Ms. Wright, why should we encourage schools to include your, let's say, world geography lessons in their curriculum?" asked the first publisher.

"I've spent my entire career in the travel industry," I began. "I have always believed that traveling abroad helps connect us with our global family. One thing we've learned in this pandemic is that what affects one area of the world can rapidly affect every corner of the globe. We've learned that we are all connected; we all share the same planet and many of the same concerns."

"I'm not entirely sure many students want to know about people in other parts of the world. What's the incentive to expand world studies?" asked the second publisher.

"There's so much fear and mistrust in our world today. In some ways, I feel we as a global family are more alienated than ever before. Knowing about other people, their culture, and their lands will help bring us all closer together. It will help break down the walls that separate us and make our children better citizens of the world."

"You make some compelling arguments, Ms. Wright," said publisher number three. "You've given us much to consider."

"What other countries do you intend to write about?" asked publisher number four.

"I have nearly completed a book on Japan, an area I know well," I answered. "My plans include books on China, India, Mexico, Brazil, Argentina, and the British Isles. Eventually, I think I could work my way around the globe."

"That's very ambitious," said the fifth member of the publishing team. "How long will this take?"

"Based on my progress so far, I think I could complete at least three, maybe four books a year," I answered.

"Ambitious indeed," commented the first publisher. "But I think it's doable, based on what I've seen so far. We are certainly interested. We like your writing style. We'll be getting back in touch with you. Do you have an agent?"

"Not yet," I said.

"You may want to consider that," he told me.

Click. The call was over. I was in business. Even though we didn't have a formal agreement, I knew only paperwork was left to seal the deal. I felt so good I thought I might just float off the chair. A few months ago, I thought my career was over for good. Now I had a new purpose. Not only a new purpose, but a whole new career. And this one would not require a lot of travel or managing an office full of people. This new career would allow me to work from home and be a wife, a mother, and a daughter while building a successful career. I felt like I was home.

The good feeling didn't last long. Korie's husband Geoff called to say Korie had tested positive for the virus. She had to be isolated from the family, even more so than before. Geoff asked if the two boys could stay with us while she was experiencing symptoms. They had been living with his parents while Korie was working in the hospital with virus patients, but now they wanted them even more removed. Geoff would be going to his house several times a day to check on Korie, and he would have some level of exposure. It was a crazy difficult situation. Of course, I said yes. Nathan quickly agreed, but where we would put everyone was another issue. My mother was in the maid's room, and Nathan's office occupied the only guest room. That left the kids' bedrooms. Time for a quick family meeting. With everyone settled on the sofa, I began.

"Aunt Korie has contracted the virus. While she is sick and contagious, Henry and James are going to stay with us."

"Terrific!" shouted Oliver. "I never get to see them. They're so much fun."

"But where will they sleep?" asked Katlin, the more practical one. "We don't have any spare bedrooms."

"You know," said my mother, concern flashing across her face, "when I was young, no one ever had their own bedrooms. It was common for four or five siblings to sleep in the same room, sometimes in the same bed."

"Ugh, gross," said Katlin.

"Pajama party!" said Oliver.

"My suggestion is that Oliver will sleep in Katlin's room while they're here, and your cousins will sleep in Oliver's room."

"He's not sleeping in my bed!" shouted Katlin. "There's no room for him."

"Good point," said Nathan calmly. "But we could get a blow-up bed for Oliver. And one for James too. How does that sound?"

"That sounds like fun," said Oliver. "But why can't I sleep in my room with my cousins?"

"If he's in my room, he better not touch anything," Katlin snapped.

"What do you have in your room that is more precious than a brother?" my mother asked. "Remember, the Bible says, where your treasure is, there is your heart too. Is your 'stuff' where your heart is, Katlin?" Boy, did my mother have a way of getting a point through to the kids. Katlin could not argue with that.

"Fine, just leave my stuff alone."

"I don't think this will be for very long," I told them. "Hopefully Aunt Korie will be well in two weeks and James and Henry can go home."

"Do they have to?" sighed Oliver. He certainly gets an A for enthusiasm.

The next morning, bright and early, Geoff was at our door with his two boys. They had each packed two bags, one with clothes and one with toys. They ran in all excited. After a quick hug with their grandma, they ran off to find their cousins. Daisy was happily running with them. She was glad to have more kids to play with.

"How is Korie?" my mother asked.

"She's not too sick," he said. "But it's early days. We're praying for a quick recovery."

"Me too," said my mother. "Lots of prayers."

"I hate that she's all alone in that house," Geoff sniffed. "She promised that she'd call if things got bad, but you know her. She wants to be a hero."

"She is a hero. She's been on the front line of this awful virus for so long. I'm sure she's saved many lives," I told him. "But this family has already lost one hero. We don't want to lose another."

I saw Geoff's eyes start to redden and rushed forward to give him a hug. "I should stay six feet apart," he said quickly. "But thank you for that, anyway."

"What can we do for you?" my mother asked.

"Maybe make some chicken soup for Korie, or something else she'd like. You can put it on the front porch and ring the doorbell, but don't stay until she comes out. Or at least, stand more than six feet away.

"One more thing," Geoff added rather sheepishly. "About school. I know we're rather across town, but could you take the boys to school? I'd hate for them to miss so much."

"We'll see to it," Nathan promised. Geoff left.

I looked at Nathan. "They go to a Lutheran School. They've been going to school in person this whole school year. That makes them more at risk than our kids. I'm not sure how our pod will like this."

"Oh, the pod," Nathan said. "That complicates matters."

And it did. Our pod family was not comfortable sharing space with children who had been exposed going to in-person school, even though there had never been a case of the virus at James's and Henry's school. We decided to disband the pod until Korie's children were gone for two weeks. We all agreed to get a virus test to make sure we didn't have it before we continued school in our pod. For now, we would continue with the kids' virtual learning classes individually. It was a hard pill to swallow, but we had to do what we had to do. I had decided some time ago to respect how others managed this crazy time. I didn't much like the people who refused to wear a mask in crowded spaces, but everybody has to decide the best way to navigate this trying issue. No one can force another person to see their point of view. But we can stay six feet away from them.

Our kids were having a great time with their cousins, but driving the boys to and from school each day was a challenge. It took about thirty minutes each way, depending on traffic, equaling about two hours a day on the road. The good part was that with so many people either working from home or not working, the traffic was pretty light. On the fourth day when I dropped the boys off, the principal came out to greet me.

"It's so good of you to keep Korie's and Geoff's boys with you and bring them to school. It must be taxing on you," he said. "They are a much-loved part of our church and school family. What can we do to help?"

"I won't lie," I said, "the back and forth to school has been a challenge. My husband is working from home and my children are attending school virtually. But my mother is with us to help."

"The moms in our school group would like to offer to help with the driving, and maybe bring you and your family some meals," he said with the sweetest smile.

I thought for a minute. Meals were really no problem, but the afternoon pickup was wearing on me. "If anyone would like to bring the boys back to us a few times, that would be a great help," I told him. "If someone would like to make a meal for Korie and Geoff, that would be appreciated."

"We would be more than happy to do that. I have your number—Geoff gave it to us when he said they would be staying with you. I'll let you know if we have some volunteers."

"Thank you so much," I replied. "That would be wonderful. God bless you."

As I drove off, I thought, the one thing this awful virus and all the events of this lost year did not take from us was our humanity. These people I've never met, in this church I've never attended, were reaching out to help us. Tears of joy rolled down my cheeks, knowing there is still good in this world.

On my way home, I stopped at a grocery store near the school to pick up a few essentials for our growing family. It was astounding how much those four kids could eat. Lunches alone were costing a fortune, as it seemed the price of everything was going up. We needed more toilet paper, napkins, and a barrel of fruit and fruit snacks and juice. My mother had been a great help. It was almost like having a real maid in the maid's room. She had prepared a list of supplies we would need, and I could hardly see over the mountain of groceries piled in my cart as I strode to the checkout. I was almost used to grocery shopping in a mask, but waiting in a long line six feet apart for the checkout was annoying. The rules in this store included that you could only approach a checkout station when the person before you had groceries packed in the cart and had left. Then and only then would a checker wave a hand for you to approach.

I pushed my loaded cart to a raised hand and began mounting the groceries onto the conveyor belt. I was nearly done when I looked up at the checker and right into the eyes of Megan. Even in her full mask, I knew who it was. Yes, *that* Megan. The Megan who slept with my husband. The Megan who came to my house and caused a scene right out of a cheap novel. That Megan. I think we stared at each other for a full three minutes. So many thoughts ran through my head. Fortunately, I didn't have any weapons. Then last week's virtual sermon popped into those wicked thoughts. "Do not judge or you, too, will be judged. Why do you look at the speck of sawdust in your brother's eye and pay no attention to the plank in your own eye?" Wasn't Megan my "brother" too? Didn't I have a massive plank in my eye? Wasn't she the Megan who handled the details of my personal and professional life for so many years? I would have reached my hand to shake hers, but there was a plexiglass shield safely protecting checkers from germs like mine.

So instead, I said, "Hello, Megan. How are you?" Then I literally held my breath waiting to see what she would do next. Memories of our last encounter made me take a step back.

"I'm doing well," she answered. Maybe smiling. Behind the masks, who could tell. "As you see, I've changed professions, but I'm quite happy with my new career."

"You were a very good office manager," I told her. "I bet you're really good at this too."

"There have been no complaints. I like it. I get to meet lots of interesting people. I picked a store far from your neighborhood, so I'm surprised to see you."

"My sister lives nearby. I was taking her kids to school," I said. "I'm glad to see you're doing well." I smiled, but again the mask prevented her from seeing, or maybe she could tell. In any case, I was soon packed in nearly twenty plastic bags since reusable bags were no longer allowed. Just another annoying rule because of the virus; I feared for the environment. I wish that was my only thought as I drove home. I

144

supposed I needed to tell Nathan of this encounter. We were trying to be completely honest with each other. We promised each other no more secrets. So, so much on our plate. I wasn't sure we could handle one more.

As I stumbled into the house with my twenty grocery bags, I saw a terrified look on my mother's face. "They've taken Korie to the hospital in an ambulance," she said, tears running down her face. "It seems she's gotten worse and was having trouble breathing. Geoff promised to call with any changes."

I dropped the bags on the floor and ran to her. We hugged, and I said, "Let's say a prayer together." We did. Sitting on the floor, we prayed for Korie and the doctors treating her. It was a hard day. Memories of my father going to the hospital filled my head. As promised, a family from Korie's church brought the boys home. I met them at the car, and as they ran into our house, I told the lovely lady driver the news.

"I will put together a prayer chain to pray for Mrs. Lewis," she said, tears welling in her eyes. "Your sister is a brave and lovely lady."

"I know, and thank you. I'll tell Geoff when he calls next. And if I have any news, I'll call the school."

My next task would be one of the hardest of this whole damn year. I had to tell James and Henry that their mother was in the hospital. They asked to pray with me. I should have expected that. After all, they went to a Christian school.

When we finished our prayer, James said, "Mommy will be alright. God will take care of her." Henry nodded. Then they ran off to play. I thought, *If only we all had such faith. Please, God, let it be so.*

James was right. God did take care of Korie. There were now better treatments for the virus. More people were recovering. But not all. The death toll was still rising. Korie was one of the lucky ones. She recovered. She spent two weeks in the hospital, and when she was out of danger, Geoff brought her home. We stood outside her house with signs, banners, and balloons welcoming her home. I think half of her church was there too. You could hardly drive down the street for all the cars, people outside of them waving signs and banners. Korie looked terribly weak but smiled at all the fuss. It would be another two weeks before she was strong enough for the boys to return home, and those two weeks would include Christmas. Henry and James would miss their mom at Christmas, but our Christmas would be larger than we had expected.

There would be no sparkling parties and fancy dresses. No caterers, no house full of people we barely knew. It would be just family. Close family. Family who had been through so much in the last year. Family we knew so much better than a year ago.

My mother insisted we all dress in our Sunday best to "attend" the virtual Christmas Eve service. It was a lovely service, and we all sang the Christmas carols. Even Nathan. My mother made her famous lasagna for Christmas Eve dinner. It was better than any five-star restaurant. We had decided to open presents that came in the mail from other grandparents. Both Geoff's and Nathan's parents watched on FaceTime. Geoff kissed each of his boys good night, gathered the dinner lovingly packed for Korie, and returned home.

Once all the kids were tucked safely in bed, Nathan and I sat by the glowing tree and shared a bottle of wine. Sitting between the roaring fire and the dazzling Christmas tree, Nathan wrapped his arm around me. I felt warm and loved.

"Not quite like last year's holiday," he said, chuckling. "No glittering parties and hordes of work friends."

"Oh yeah. I saw Megan last week," I said. Nathan immediately sat up and dropped his arm. I didn't want to break the charm of this evening, but I had been holding this in too long.

"She didn't accost you again, did she?" he asked with concern in his eyes.

"No, she was working as a checker at the grocery store near the boys' school. She was pleasant and seemed happy."

"That's good news, I suppose. I guess checker is a step down, but it pays well enough. You accosted her, did you?" he asked, smiling.

"Almost," I answered honestly. "I actually thought about it, but then I remembered the sermon about judging. You know, the dust in another's eye when there's a log in your own?"

"Oh, yeah, that's pretty convicting. Would it help if I said again how sorry I am?" he asked.

"Would it help if I said the same?" We looked in each other's eyes. They held love but also pain. "I'm so glad we're together again, Nathan, but I think we have more healing to do. Maybe next year we should seek out a counselor who will help us through some of our issues."

"I expect you're right. Just sweeping it under the rug and moving on never fixed anything. But I do like where we are now."

"Me too," I said, and we kissed with a year's worth of pent-up passion. Nathan took me by the hand and led me upstairs. So much better than last year. We faced each other honestly, with no secrets.

Geoff joined us for Christmas breakfast. My mother has never allowed presents to be opened before we eat. I think it's a German thing. When the dishes were cleared, we retreated to the living room. The massive pile of presents under our tree was a bounty of delicious excess. It's amazing what you can find on a budget if you know where to look. Before we began to open the gifts, my mother read the Christmas story so we would all remember the real reason for the season. I gave each child a gift to open. Glittering red and green paper flew through the room. I knew I had purchased the right gifts this year because I'd listened to my children. Really listened. The euphoria of opening presents lasted less than an hour. The kids all retreated to their corners to play with sparkling new toys, and Geoff returned to Korie with a box of goodies prepared by my mom.

I set to my challenge for the day. I decided to take my cooking skills to a new height. For dinner we would have prime rib, duchess potatoes, and bûche de Noël. I saw someone make it on TV, and I'd been determined to give it a try. It's a European Christmas tradition of chocolate cake rolled around cream and iced to look like a log. It was finished with mushrooms made of meringue and rosemary stems that looked like twigs. It was a masterpiece. I brought it to the table amid cheers and applause. I had worked on it all week, and it was well worth it. It tasted as good as it looked. The kids loved it. Turns out, eating a log is lots of fun.

Four days after Christmas, James and Henry went home. Our house seemed quiet. Our kids missed their cousins, but they had a plethora of new toys to distract them.

While the kids were playing with their new toys, I was digging through my old work files to find some information on my next booklet when a paper fell out of a file. I picked it up and saw my 2020 New Year's resolutions. I chuckled a little as I read through them:

1. Spend more time with my kids.
2. Spend more time with my husband.
3. Stop Oliver from throwing tantrums.
4. Help Katlin navigate the bullies at school.
5. Figure out why Megan is so concerned about Nathan.
6. Find a new dimension to my career.

What a difference a year makes. I had—or rather, the pandemic had—accomplished goals one and two. I had made progress on resolutions three and four, far more than I would have without the pandemic. How could I have ever predicted all the changes 2020 would bring to my life? It was truly a year of loss. I lost my job, my career, my father, and nearly my sister and my marriage. My kids lost their school. Our pod was no real substitute for learning in a classroom full of other children. But next to those losses were many things found. I found a new career, I hoped. I found new friends in our pod. I found a church family. I learned to cook, clean, and plant a garden. My marriage was on more solid ground than it had been in years. Yes, we struggled to meet the budget, and life had more challenges. But I knew we would never go back to the life of glitter, lies, and delusions we had before the pandemic. Much was lost, but much was found.

By the end of December, close to 20,000,000 Americans had been infected with the virus. In December, 95,000 people were in hospitals struggling for their lives due to the virus. At the end of 2020, the American death toll from the virus stood at 432,000. The worldwide death toll stood at over three million. This virus had proven the deadliest in recorded history. And it wasn't over.

Even without the virus, 2020 would have looked apocalyptic. Earthquakes shook Turkey, the Caribbean, China, Iran, Russia, the Philippines, and India. A volcano erupted in the Philippines, and locust swarms devastated crops in East Africa and parts of India and Asia. Cyclone Amphan hit India and Bangladesh. Europe was struck by extratropical cyclones Ciara and Alex, costing nearly $6 billion and killing thirty people. Floods affected people in India, Japan, and China. And in Australia, brushfires had started in December and were showing no signs of slowing down. Before they were over, they would burn about 18.6 million hectares, destroy over 5,900 buildings, and kill thirty-four people. Another 400 people died due to the residual smoke inhalation.

In the U.S., there were a record-breaking twenty-two separate billion-dollar weather and climate disasters. Those events included a record seven tropical cyclones, thirteen severe storms, a drought, and wildfires. At one time, it seemed like the whole West Coast from Mexico to Washington state was ablaze. A record four million acres burned across California—double the previous record. Five of California's top six largest wildfires ever burned between August and September.

In the northeast and the western half of the U.S., drought conditions expanded or intensified across much of this area: 43 percent of the contiguous U.S. was officially in drought.

Let's not forget the historic derecho storm that traveled 770 miles from South Dakota to Ohio, producing widespread winds greater than 100 mph. The derecho caused severe damage to homes, businesses, vehicles, and crops along its path. In northeastern Illinois, including the Chicago metropolitan area, there were fifteen tornadoes. Even in St. Louis, we felt the derecho winds, although not as severely as in other states.

Now for the good news—no, the great news. On December 11, the first authorized vaccine for this virus in the U.S. was approved by the Food and Drug Administration (FDA) for emergency use. The authorization for this two-dose vaccine came a day after the FDA advisory committee voted seventeen to four to give the vaccine a greenlight. The vaccine was manufactured by Pfizer-BioNTech. The company announced that it would immediately begin shipping vaccines from their three manufacturing facilities in the U.S. One was in St. Louis. The first recipients of the vaccines would be the elderly patients in nursing homes who had been decimated by the virus and health care workers who were exposed daily. Moderna was completing the Phase 3 trial of its virus vaccine and it would be approved shortly. There was a light at the end of the tunnel. It was a dim light, but still, a light. Many more infections and deaths would occur before the majority of people were vaccinated, but hope is a powerful emotion. Where there is hope, there is life, and we were ever grateful for all we had retained and gained in this lost year.

# January 2021 – Terror in the Capitol

Our New Year's celebration was nothing like 2020. The glitz and glamour of the Zodiac Room at the Chase Park Plaza were replaced by a simple family celebration at home. All of last year's party venues and even most restaurants were still closed due to the pandemic. Instead of midnight in a shimmering gown, it was PJs by the fireplace with Nathan. I splurged on steak for dinner that the adults shared, including my mother. Our kids had chicken nuggets per their request. I planned on humiliating them with this choice at their weddings.

I had ordered a box of New Year's fun from the internet. (What would a pandemic be without online ordering?) The box included hats, noisemakers, exploding confetti poppers, and simple firecrackers. We celebrated with the kids at 10 p.m., which was extremely late for them, and sent them off to bed. I think this was the first time in many years (if ever) that our children were included in our New Year's celebration. Probably the first time ever with my mother, who was just as glad as the kids to retire to her room by 10:30. That left Nathan and me with some much-needed together time. We talked, really talked, with full-on honesty. No more secrets. No more lies. We vowed all over again to put our past mistakes behind us and look to the future. That illusive future. What would it bring? We discussed the kids. I had recently made an appointment to have Oliver tested for ADHD and dyslexia. After spending so much time with him in the last few months, I was pretty sure what it would show. We both agreed knowing was better than not knowing. St. Louis County had abundant resources for children with learning disabilities. We hoped it would make Oliver stronger. With their support, he would move past his reading problems and find school more tolerable.

Katlin was flourishing both academically and socially without the presence of the bully, whom we had identified. I had already requested that whenever they went back to school in person, Katlin would not be in the bully's class. Not too surprisingly, I learned several other parents had requested the same thing. I had prayed for her and her parents. They had a tough road ahead.

We talked about Nathan's career. His company had already decided, as many U.S. companies had, not to go back to the office as usual. My brother Adam, who had moved to Seattle for a job at Boeing, had only been to his office once, and there were no plans to go back to working in the office. Many companies had discovered they could save a bundle on office space with employees working from home. Surprisingly, workers proved to be more productive working from home. Even with wandering children, there were fewer distractions at home. No more wasting time with long chats at the water cooler. No more long, sometimes liquid lunches. No more traffic tie-ups to make workers late. And, I might add, no more office romances causing all manner of trouble. A decade ago, anyone asking to work from home for personal reasons would have swiftly been dismissed. Now it was preferred—one of many things this pandemic had changed, at least for the foreseeable future.

We talked about my career. My brother had recently asked me to serve as a translator for his work. It took almost no time. I simply attended a Zoom meeting with several people from Adam's office and a team from Japan. When each side spoke, they paused as I translated. It worked very well. They completed a deal, and I was paid extremely well for my time. Adam said I could become a preferred vendor if my company had a legal name. That wasn't hard. I simply filed a name with the state, and I had a translation company called Roni Speaks. Not very creative, I knew, but it worked. I had two more Zoom meetings set up with Adam's company and two with the Japanese customer and other companies. This was the most work I had ever contracted with so little effort. Adam assured me that there was a need for translation work and the potential for me to be successful. He suggested I look into hiring translators for other languages. It was an appealing business. I could do it all from home because nobody was traveling, especially not abroad, and most business meetings were taking place over Zoom anyway. All I needed was to keep the noise away from my computer during a call. That was a little more difficult than it sounds. If I managed to distract the kids, then Daisy decided to bark. I decided to make a space in the basement where I could bar the door for my Zoom calls. I put up a bookshelf for a background. We had plenty of books that needed a shelf. Finding a shelving unit, like all things during the pandemic, wasn't easy, but I managed.

Nathan and I sipped champagne and talked about all these new challenges. One unknown was when the kids would go back to school in person. My mother was managing much of the online learning, but I think it was wearing on her. Katlin was managing the online work pretty well, but Oliver was always a challenge. I tried to be the guide for most of his classes, but I now had more of my own work. It was too cold now to continue the pod outside, and most of the parents weren't comfortable with sending their kids into other homes. Even with the vaccines rolling out, the hold the pandemic had over our lives seemed a long way from lifting.

We finally gave up discussing all these heavy issues and gave into our desire to celebrate the New Year in a personal way. Nathan put out the fire and led me upstairs. Sometime later, I fell asleep in his arms feeling truly loved. I know there was much that needed to be resolved, but so much more was clear. We loved each other and our family, and we would find a way to make it all work.

The first week of January went by quickly. The weather was fairly mild for January in St. Louis, but we would pay for that later. Oliver had his evaluation for ADHD and dyslexia. The test was on Zoom, as was everything else in our life. I was pretty sure of the results since I had to coax him out from under the desk several times during the test. He was bored to death (or rather, my death) with the testing process. I was pretty much out of ideas for keeping him in the chair and focused on a Zoom screen. His teachers all had some creative ideas, but honestly, even I got bored sometimes. There's only so much one can do to hold a child's attention on a live video lesson. He needed more activity, but that was hard in the middle of winter with every indoor activity closed.

On January 6, I had a rare day free of Zoom calls and my new projects, so I set out to stock up on groceries. Most grocery staples were plentiful now, but prices had skyrocketed. I rushed to the store to get grapefruits, two dollars each, then stood staring at the sign. How was it, I wondered, that a two-dollar grapefruit was a rare bargain? Lemons were sixty cents each. Don't get me started on meat. Prices had been rising all year. Was I the only one who noticed? And environmentally friendly options, like reusable grocery bags, were out the window too. A year ago, we considered plastic bottles and bags as environmental disasters. Now, we had no choice.

All these issues were swirling in my head as I drove home. The phone rang, bringing me back to the real world. It was Grace. I hadn't talked to her since before the holidays.

"Hello, Grace. How was your holiday?"

"Forget the holiday, Roni. Have you seen what's happening in Washington?"

"I'm just driving home from a shopping expedition," I told her. "I'm so appalled at the price of everything."

"Well, get ready to be more appalled. Trump supporters are storming the Capitol, demanding that Vice President Pence stop the electoral vote count and declare Trump the winner. They're destroying the Capitol building."

"No, nothing like that could happen in the United States. It isn't possible. I know President Trump refuses to acknowledge that he lost, but we have a democracy. We have due process. He can't force his way into the presidency. He just can't."

"Get home and turn on your TV. You'll see. This is insane," Grace said.

I got home as quickly as I could. My mother and Nathan were sitting at the TV transfixed. They had sent Katlin and Oliver to their rooms, telling them it was a free-screen day, meaning they could play games on their tablets as long as they wanted until further notice. What I saw on the TV turned my stomach to mush. Vast crowds of riotous, violent men and women wearing all manner of strange attire were smashing windows and streaming into the Capitol. Our sacred national capitol building was being torn apart.

The news reporter said the joint session of Congress had convened to count electoral votes to formalize Joe Biden's presidential victory. Thousands of supporters of President Donald Trump had gathered in the Ellipse in Washington D.C. for a "Save America" rally. Ever since the election results were reported by the news media, President Trump had insisted the election was a fraud and Biden's victory was false. He claimed that the election had been stolen from him, and he was demanding that Vice President Pence and Congress reject Biden's legal victory. He told the crowd, "If you don't fight like hell, you're not going to have a country anymore."

An angry mob of thousands left the Ellipse and marched to the Capitol, quickly overpowering the Capitol Police and breaking into the building, chanting "Hang Mike Pence!" and other violent rantings. They continued to vandalize and loot the House and Senate offices for hours while President Trump refused to call out the National Guard to stop them. Capitol Police bravely evacuated the Senate and House of

Representative chambers and directed the lawmakers to safety while rioters chanted for their demise and ransacked the empty chambers.

I watched in disbelief. I had wondered if President Trump would ever leave the White House. I had visions of uniformed guards dragging him from the building, or him barricading himself within and refusing to allow the new president entry. But this? Never this. The only word to describe what was happening was "insurrection." How could this happen in the United States of America? It violated every single fundamental law of the Founding Fathers. The one overriding principle that had always defined democracy was our free, open, and honest elections followed by a peaceful transfer of power. If one man could simply refuse to accept the decision of the American people and declare the election invalid, this was no longer a democracy. From that time on, nothing in politics would ever make sense again.

I watched in horror as the vicious mob ransacked the offices of members of Congress. Rioters threw private documents in the air and smashed or stole personal possessions. I snuggled close to Nathan, burying my head in his shoulder.

"How can this be happening in our country? How?" I asked.

"I don't have an answer," he said, holding me close. "It's just total insanity. So much hatred. So much violence. I can hardly watch."

"I'm in shock," my mother added. "My eyes see what's happening, but my brain just can't comprehend it. It's like something from a horrible doomsday movie, or some fictional end of the world. Just not our Capitol. I can't understand what these people think they'll accomplish and how can they be so filled with hate."

"President Trump must be responsible," Nathan added. "His constant ranting about the election being fraudulent and stolen has stirred this anger to boiling."

"But whatever they do, short of a coup, would not change the elections results, right?" I asked.

After some time, my mother got up and shut off the TV. "I can't handle any more of this," she said. "I don't think it will do you any good to continue to watch. Perhaps play a game with the kids or take a walk. It's not that cold. Tear yourself away, for a while at least. I'm sure there will be much more, about these wretched events, but we need to clear our minds."

She was right. We all bundled up and took a walk. It was amazing how peaceful the evening was. No riots here. No violent mobs. Just crisp cool air with a setting sun. The walk did us a world of good. As we walked, we tried to explain to our kids what had happened, but words failed. I'm sure we did a poor job of it, but what words could describe this mayhem to children? They needed to know, but we didn't want to scare them. That was hard. We were scared. We were terrified. We not only had a pandemic, social injustice, and apocalyptic weather to deal with, but now a political revolt too? Surely not!

After the kids were tucked into bed, I continued to watch the never-ending coverage of the Capitol riots. I saw no arrests, although we were told one rioter was killed by police. When it was over, five people were dead and 140 injured. Once police managed to clear the Capitol building of rioters, the members of Congress that had taken shelter returned to the chamber and continued counting the electoral votes. In the early morning hours of January 7, Vice President Pence declared President-elect Biden and Vice President-elect Kamala Harris as victors. Later President Trump committed to an orderly transition of power on January 20 without ever conceding defeat or congratulating his opponent. Orderly maybe, but it was a long way from cordial or even civil. I had so many images in my head of other past presidents jovially escorting newly elected presidents and their families around the White House. Nothing like that would happen in this most bizarre year.

It was a little hard getting back to real life after this unreal episode. Whatever I tried to do, my mind kept turning back to those images of a mob breaking into and damaging our nation's sacred Capitol building. It didn't help that every new report had pictures of the events, forcing us to live it over and over.

But life did go on. My kids were doing virtual school at home without the pod. They each had their own schedule of Zoom classes. Neither of them went without complaint, but Oliver more than Katlin. I was trying to follow what was going on with their classes. My mother was a huge help. I just couldn't imagine how a large family kept it all straight. We had no word yet on returning to in-person classes. Infection rates had soared since the holidays. Many blamed it on holiday family gatherings. Whatever the cause, hospitals across the country had reached near capacity. Ventilators were in high demand, and doctors and nurses were stretched to exhaustion. It was a new year but not much had changed. We still had to wear masks wherever we went, at least in St. Louis County. Restaurants, bars, gyms, and nearly every entertainment venue were still closed. Those that were open had strict limitations. Wherever I went, I was reminded to keep six feet apart with no personal contact.

Eating takeout at home had become standard. We hardly remembered going out to eat in a restaurant. It seemed like a long distant memory.

I think the whole nation was holding its collective breath for January 20, Inauguration Day. No one—I expect not even those closest to the president—knew what he would do. Our kids were hard at work, or at least making an effort, at virtual school while Nathan, my mother, and I watched the TV with bated breath. President Trump left the White House early in the day before any activities had begun. He never greeted the incoming president or acknowledged him in any way.

"I can't remember an inauguration in our history where the current president has not attended the ceremony," my mother said.

"I expect all those in attendance are happy to avoid him. Especially Vice President Pence since the Trump supporters were building gallows to hang him," Nathan said.

"I'm just glad he's gone with no more drama," I said. "I honestly didn't think he'd ever leave."

"I don't expect him to go quietly into the night," Nathan said. "Maybe our politicians can now tone down the viperous rhetoric."

"Don't hold your breath," I replied. "I think there's plenty of venom left in Washington."

That may well have been, but it was not on display on that day's ceremony. Although much was missing—the crowds, the bands, and the parades—those in attendance were elegantly dressed and cordial. Past Presidents Bill Clinton, George W. Bush, and Barack Obama were as gracious as ever. The speeches were full of civility, hope, and talk of vaccines. The music was lovely and, oh, the poem. It brought tears, not fears, to my eyes.

January concluded without much drama. Vaccines were being administered to a select group of elderly and medical workers. We saw dark days, but still, there was hope. It wasn't over yet. By the end of January, just under 26,000,000 cases of the virus had been confirmed in the U.S. The hospitals were filled to capacity with 95,000 patients fighting for their lives. The death toll in the U.S. now exceeded a staggering 432,000.

# February 2021 –
# Baby, It's Cold

February began with lots of hope. Hope of a vaccine that would put an end to this awful pandemic and return our old world to us after a whole year of missing out on so much. The pandemic had ruled over our lives and kept us from doing so many of the things we loved, kept our children from going to school, and kept us from our chosen careers. It kept us from socializing, entertainment, and sports. It kept us from traveling and from loved ones. It kept us from the life we wanted to live. We were virtually locked in our homes with only immediate family. All the rest had to stay six feet apart. I, for one, was sick of six feet.

But I spoke of hope. Ugh! Thoughts of the pandemic and what I had missed invaded my brain yet again. The hope was the vaccine. Not just one vaccine, but possibly three vaccines. They all had problems. Some had to be kept at ridiculously low temperatures, and all were approved only for emergency use. Well, hello, this was an emergency. But emergency use meant it couldn't be distributed like other vaccines to doctors and pharmacies. This special vaccine was distributed in places you would never expect to go for medical care, that's how special it was. And the government controlled who got the vaccine, when, and where. The national government—I really never understood who was in charge— distributed the vaccines with their eternal wisdom to state governments, who in turn distributed to counties or wherever they deemed was most in need. Each state's governor was in charge of distributing the vaccine in that state. It was very arbitrary with few consistent rules across states.

People were put in categories depending on age and occupation. You could only get the vaccine if your group was eligible. Frontline medical workers and nursing home workers and patients were in the first group. As a frontline pandemic worker, my sister was eligible in the first wave of vaccines. My mother, who was over sixty-seven, would be in the second wave, theoretically. We hoped she could get the vaccine soon.

Supply was extremely limited. Even if you qualified, there may not be enough vaccine in your area. Finding out where the vaccine was available was extremely difficult. I registered my mother online in every place you could possibly register, but no vaccine was available. People without internet access or know-how had no way to register for the vaccine. We lived in one of the most heavily populated counties in Missouri, but St. Louis County got very little supply. It was reported that some rural counties in Missouri got more vaccine doses than they had people. Because the vaccine had short expiration dates and required extreme low temperatures, some vaccine was wasted if too much was sent to places with too few eligible people. I knew people so desperate for a vaccine that they were driving across the state or to another state to get it. It seemed like idiots were running the show, and nobody had any idea what was going on.

On a brighter note, my kids were going back to school. Our school district announced that children who wanted to return to school could do so the second week of February on a limited basis. Each class could only have half the normal number of students, carefully placed—you guessed it—six feet apart. No group gatherings like recess or lunch time. Half of the students would go to school in the morning and half in the afternoon. Fortunately, both of my kids were going in the afternoon. The school was making an effort to schedule all children from the same family in school at the same time, but it was all so terribly difficult. Parents could choose to continue at-home learning. Crazy, right? Well, school was important, and I was delighted for whatever in-person school time our kids had. Teachers were now tasked with teaching in school and online at the same time. I'm not sure how they stayed sane.

Back to the hope part. So far it had been a fairly mild winter. No terrible life-changing weather events around the country. In St. Louis, we usually get our coldest weather at the beginning of January, and that had passed with no weather-related incidents. I fully believed that 2021 would be a completely different year with none of the drama of 2020. Boy, was I wrong!

Instead of getting warmer in February, it was getting colder. We knew cold in St. Louis and weren't too concerned about it. As Valentine's Day approached, the temperature kept going down and down. But still, we managed to celebrate. Of all the things the pandemic took from us, it also gave: It gave our family a new closeness. We told one another how much we loved each other every day. Valentine's Day seemed to be a good time to celebrate our new closeness. I ordered a special little gift for each family member. I got my mother a new winter shawl to keep her warm all the time. I got each of the kids a special snuggly stuffy, as Oliver would say—stuffed animal to everyone else. I got Nathan a beautifully framed picture of our family I'd had taken during Christmas, and a better desk light for his office. I even got a new chew toy for Daisy. It was a necessity—she had chewed through almost all the other toys and some things that weren't toys. None of the gifts were very expensive, but all were personal and given with a loving spirit.

I planned a special dinner of roast chicken with mashed potatoes, something the whole family liked. In place of a salad, I made little red gelatin hearts surrounded by berries. It was so pretty. Oliver helped with the gelatin. Katlin helped me make a red velvet heart-shaped cake. Thank you, Internet, for the cake pan. Thank you, Martha Stewart, for the recipe. We covered the cake with chocolate icing and little heart candies. Both kids helped decorate the cake. My mother helped with the chicken and mashed potatoes. It was truly a family effort. Katlin and Oliver made heart placemats for the table. Nathan brought my mother and I each a bouquet of colorful flowers. No roses. We didn't have the money for that. But the carnations and baby's breath were lovely and helped make our table festive. I even brought out my fancy china. It was a bit risky with Oliver, but we all learned life was precious and short. Use the good china as often as possible. It makes any meal festive.

When we were all seated, Nathan led the family in a special Valentine's prayer. It was all so beautiful. So Norman Rockwell. It was hard to believe this was my family. I don't think I had ever celebrated Valentine's Day with my children before. Nathan and I would go to a fancy restaurant while the nanny ordered pizza for the kids. We laughed together and shared our hopes and fears. I couldn't quite explain the tears running down my face. A year ago, I might have expected a gold bracelet from Nathan when I didn't deserve it and he didn't want to give it. Today I got an inexpensive bouquet of flowers and was happier than ever. So very much was lost in the pandemic. One chair was forever empty. Our lives had forever changed, but much was gained too. At least in our family, we were moving toward a better chapter.

Then it got colder. Much colder. Record-breaking colder. Not just in St. Louis, but all over. Our temperature hit two degrees. That's not counting the wind chill. And it snowed. We hadn't seen measurable snow in quite a while, but this was significant snowfall. We got nearly eight inches between Monday and Tuesday.

Tuesday morning, we woke up to water dripping from the kitchen ceiling. We guessed a pipe had broken somewhere in the bathroom plumbing, probably in the master bath. My mother suggested I quickly fill the largest pots with water before turning off the water to the house. I tried to convince Oliver and Katlin to continue their virtual lessons, but too much was going on. Nathan was calling every plumber in a twenty-mile radius. None was available for at least a week. Apparently, every old house in the St. Louis area also had frozen, busted plumbing. We had to wait in a long line.

We couldn't stay here with no plumbing. There were five of us and three bathrooms. We needed plumbing. My mother suggested we might be able to stay at her house in Washington, but the roads were snow-covered and treacherous. A hotel wasn't a good option in a pandemic. Besides, we were barely making ends meet. A weeklong hotel stay was not in the budget. The only other idea I had was Korie's house. It wasn't quite as big as ours, but it did have four bedrooms and a foldout bed in the basement. It was a little further than I liked to drive after a snowstorm, but I thought we could make it. I called Korie, and she said she'd be delighted for us to come. I'm sure "delighted" didn't capture the emotion exactly, but she was willing for us to come. However, my mother had another idea.

"I'm going to stay with my friend Sarah in Webster," she informed us. "She's a widow too, and she just got this lovely new condo in a senior village. She's been telling me all about it and said she'd love for me to stay. Her son has a four-wheel drive vehicle, and he's coming to pick me up."

"You don't want to stay at Korie's?" I asked, a little bewildered and bemused.

"Please tell Korie I'd be delighted to stay with her, but I think the four of you will pretty much fill her house. Sarah's place sounds delightful, and I'd really like the opportunity to catch up with her. I miss my friends. Living here is a true blessing, but I long for my old friends." I couldn't argue with that. I missed friends too.

Next, we had to start packing. Oliver was most concerned about taking his new snuggly and didn't pack underwear or pajamas. Fortunately, I checked both of the kids' suitcases. I packed as much food as I thought we might use. I had four grocery bags full. Then I had to pack all of Daisy's necessities: food, chew toys, leash, bed. Nathan would continue to work at Korie's house, so he packed his office. We barely got it all in our too-expensive Escalade. It was days like this that I was thankful for that big gas-guzzling vehicle.

Shortly after Sarah's son came to pick up my mother, we took off for Korie's house. The snowfall was one of the biggest in recent memory. The roads were slick but passable. We did, however, see many accidents along the way. Korie's subdivision was perched on one of the many hills dotting St. Louis. We turned into her street, feeling relieved that we had made it, when the Escalade started spinning. As it spun, it swerved sideways, narrowly missing a parked car. Nathan stopped and said he couldn't go any further. We parked on the street with Korie's house in sight. Carrying our most necessary belongings, we trudged through the snow to her house. I had a suitcase in one hand and Daisy's leash in the other. She ran so fast I slipped in the snow and fell on my face.

"Are you alright, Roni?" Nathan asked, running up to me. I lifted my head, now covered in snow. Brushing snow from my mouth, I said, "Fine, I think. Just wet and cold." I must have looked hilarious because my family, in unison, burst into laughter. Bent over laughing, they each ended up falling into the snow. Somehow, we finally made it to Korie's front door. She gasped as she opened it.

"You look frightful," she said with a big smile that belied her words. "Come in and dry off." The kids and I went in while Nathan and Geoff took some sand and pushed our Escalade out of the snow and up to Korie's driveway. Once we were all inside, Korie produced a large pan of lasagna that she had made for Mardi Gras.

"Did you remember that today is Mardi Gras?" she asked. Of course I didn't remember what day it was. Water was running down the wall! Before I could answer, Korie continued, "I know lasagna is not a traditional Mardi Gras dish, but it's what my family likes. And it seemed appropriate for Fat Tuesday."

"We love lasagna," said Oliver and Katlin in unison. "Mom never makes it." *Note to self: make more lasagna.*

"Lasagna would be perfect," I said. And it was, warming us to our toes.

166

Sleeping arrangements were pretty tight. My kids took Henry's room and Henry moved in with James. One kid in each room would have to sleep on an air mattress each night. We tossed a coin to see who would go first. They alternated sleeping on the air mattress. It seemed like a good idea, but I wasn't sure how much they'd all sleep. Nathan and I had the guest room. It was a little tighter than we were used to, but it was a bed—free, safe, and warm. We were too exhausted to worry about anything. The only one who was restless was Daisy. We decided she would sleep in our room to keep the kids from playing with her all night. But even Daisy was tired. We all had a place to sleep with running water and working toilets, and we had a plan to get our plumbing fixed, even if it would take a week.

I woke early the next morning and crept to the kitchen to make breakfast for the whole gang. I found Korie was already there working on coffee.

"I thought I'd make everybody breakfast this morning," I said. "It's sort of a thank you for letting us stay. Do you like pancakes?"

"Pancakes would be wonderful," Korie replied. "With my work schedule, I rarely get a chance to make more than a bowl of cereal. The boys have a rare snow day today, so the boys will be extra excited— actually, we'll all be home. I have the day off, too."

"I think my kids will have to go to their half day of school," I told her. "Since we've only gone back part-time, I doubt that our district will declare a snow day."

"Have you looked outside?" Korie asked. "I don't think you're going anywhere, whether or not your school is closed."

I looked outside and had to agree with Korie. Their street, with its long hill, had not been plowed The roads looked worse than they had the previous night when the snow was not this deep. Venturing out in this wasn't the wisest decision.

"I have to admit, Korie, you have a good point. I think they'll be doing some virtual learning today."

"I hope you have some time to play in the snow with us. It could be a good time."

"We'll make that happen," I assured her.

Breakfast was fun. The kids enjoyed their pancakes. I used my mother's trick of sprinkling powdered sugar on the pancakes to make it "snow." They all giggled at that and gobbled up the pancakes. After breakfast, I took my kids and their tablets to the family room for online lessons. Nathan retreated to the game room in the basement to work. We struggled through work all morning, but after lunch, we bundled up and went outside to play.

Korie's boys had a great sled, and the kids took turns sliding down their big hill. Daisy went hysterical chasing snowballs. Each family built a snow fort, then we battled with snowballs. Daisy made it more funnier and more difficult as she jumped for the thrown balls. However, it didn't take long for all of us to get cold. The snow was followed by record-breaking cold, and we couldn't stay out too long. Back inside, we warmed up with hot chocolate Korie made for us. She also made my mother's fried chicken for dinner, which we all enjoyed immensely. After dinner, Geoff pulled out some interesting puzzles, and we had a family-versus-family puzzle competition. Korie's family was a little quicker putting together puzzles—these were, after all, their puzzles—but we all had a good time.

The week went by fast. Both sets of kids went to their respective schools the rest of the week. Korie's kids went all day, mine half days. The long drive wasn't fun, but we managed. I cooked as often as I could. Korie was working most days. One day, I had a nice surprise. Adam called me and asked if I could act as interpreter for a Zoom meeting he was having with a group of Japanese clients. I was happy to do it. I used Nathan's equipment in the basement game room for the meeting. It took nearly an hour. I worried that my Japanese was a little rusty, but I pulled it off without a hitch. When the meeting was over, Adam said, "You were great, Roni. We could use you a lot. We sometimes need

German interpreters too. Does Roni Speaks have a bank account where we could transfer money?"

"Money," I said, a little too surprised. "I hadn't thought about money."

"Don't say that to too many of your clients." Adam chuckled. "I think you're going to get lots of business."

"I guess I didn't think too much about it," I answered.

"Well, I think you'll get more calls."

He was right. Word of mouth turned out to be my best marketing tool. Roni Speaks continued to grow. Zoom made it so easy.

Before we knew it, the weekend was upon us. Saturday was Oliver's seventh birthday. There would be no big celebration at the Magic House like last year. The Magic House and all other such venues were still closed. But we were with family. I made Oliver's favorite chocolate cake. We all pitched in to try to clean the house on Saturday, but between the four kids and Daisy, I don't think we helped all that much.

Nathan ordered an Italian dinner for everyone from Oliver's favorite restaurant. On his way to pick up dinner, Nathan stopped by our house and found the birthday gift I had ordered for Oliver. It was a Star Wars Lego kit. Korie had found a remote-control jeep for Oliver, and he was thrilled. It was a delightful party, and I hoped we'd left Korie's family with enough leftovers for at least another meal. We ordered pizza Sunday for our last night. I knew there was no way I could ever repay Korie and Geoff for all their hospitality. But what are families for? Actually, that's just what they said when we left Monday morning. That same evening, my mother returned to us from her stay at her friend's condo with a whole new outlook on her future. That evening, after the kids had gone to bed, she came to speak to us.

"You two have been so wonderful to me," she began. "I will never be able to repay you for your kindness. I can't imagine how I would have navigated my grief by myself in that house I shared with Robert for all those years. Here, I had some purpose and loved ones always around me. Your children were the greatest comfort. However, I think it's time for me to move on. I discovered how widowhood and retirement could be in the last week with Sarah. I'm going to sell my Washington house and buy a condo in Sarah's retirement development as soon as one is available. I'll be close, but you'll have your house back."

"Oh, Mom," I cried, big tears flowing from my eyes. "I can hardly imagine being here without you. You've become such a big part of our lives."

"I won't be far. I plan to come over often. However, I would like to leave one part of me. Sarah's development doesn't allow pets. Can Daisy stay here?"

"I don't think you could pry her away from Oliver and Katlin," I said. I should have added me too. I was sad and happy all at once. It was so right for her to be here after my father's death. Just as it was so right for her to find her own way forward now. Life does go on.

The plumbers fixed our pipes Monday, leaving a big hole in the wall. But it was all fixable, and I now had two sources of income. Roni Speaks, my new business, was starting well. It didn't take too much of my time, especially since the translation work was all on Zoom. I had plenty of time to continue my "Connection with Our World." series for kids. The publisher was pleased, and I promised four books each year for a profitable sum.

After weeks of two of us enrolling Mom through numerous health care sites for the vaccine, Korie was finally able to wrangle a vaccine appointment for our mother. She was in the age group available for the current vaccine level, but we were beyond exasperated trying to get her an appointment. Somehow, I felt it was all going to end soon. But not before much more pain.

When the gaping hole in our wall was finally fixed, I felt a little like something in our lives was fixed. Nathan and I stood looking at the last of the repairs from our broken pipes.

"This old house has served us well, in good times and bad," he said. "There was a time at the beginning of this horrible pandemic when I thought we may not be able to afford this house. There were also times when I thought I may not stay."

"I know," I told him, moving in close and taking his hand. "I had some of those same thoughts. And now?"

"And now, you couldn't blast me from this place or from you and our family. I'm not sure what the future will bring, but I know we will face it together. Our new faith will see us through."

I lost so much during the pandemic of 2020, but I gained even more. My marriage was better than ever. I had a new career—make that two new careers. I knew my kids better than ever. We were making less money and our financial future wasn't as certain, but we had hope. We lost a lot of glamour from our lives, but that had never made us happy, really happy. Our new faith had made us stronger. We were better prepared to face the future, whatever it may bring. Someday, the world would return to normal—probably not ever exactly how it had been before the pandemic. Many things had changed, maybe forever. I, for one, was OK with that. Maybe we were all ready for a new post-pandemic world.

Our Valentine's winter storm was bad enough. but it was much worse in Texas. The winter storm that rocked Texas from February 11 to 20 brought not only snow, sleet, and freezing rain to southeast Texas, but also extreme cold temperatures that lasted for days. This storm was the most impactful winter event in recent history. It caused multiday road closures, power outages, loss of heat, broken pipes, and other damage across Texas. The storm shuttered oil and gas production, food processing facilities, and manufacturing plants. Millions lost power for days on end in the record cold. Many of those also experienced broken pipes, losing power and water at the same time. It was estimated that the cost of the storm could top $200 billion. That would be more than the worst of the recent hurricanes. Unlike hurricanes, which affect a more localized area, this winter storm had spread over almost the entire state of Texas. The damage to Texas's agriculture could last for several seasons. Crops froze as temperatures stayed below zero for several days. The storm destroyed tons of vegetables in the Rio Grande Valley and about half of the state's citrus harvest. The cost was felt around the country as prices of produce rose.

Even with vaccines available on a limited basis, the virus continued to cause illness and death. By the end of February, the U.S. had recorded more than 28,000,000 cases. There were 47,000 people in the U.S. hospitalized with the virus. The death toll from the virus now stood just over a half million people. There may be a light at the end of the tunnel, but the virus was certainly not done causing death and illness.

# Epilogue

Independence Day, 2021, is here at last. I've spent the last months writing down my memories of My Lost Year. I feel that it's important to remember. Or at least someday, I will want to remember the year that changed so much for me. Since I finished my recollections of that year, much has happened and not happened. We are all fully vaccinated. At least, Nathan and I are, as are just about all the adults I know. Those over twelve, the current age limit for vaccinations, are getting their first shots or waiting until they can get their second. We are hopeful that the age limit will be lowered enough for Oliver and Katlin to get a vaccine soon. We are very hopeful that this year, in-person, full-time school *will* start. Oliver received his diagnosis of ADHD and dyslexia, which I'd suspected would be the case. The diagnosis allows us access to special services. He's in summer school now, on Zoom with excellent teachers, learning to read with dyslexia. He's made huge progress. Katlin is in summer camp—yes, summer camp is open. Hallelujah! She has found new friends with no bullies. She seems to be blooming in the best way.

Most everything is open. Nathan and I actually had dinner out, inside a restaurant, with friends (all fully vaccinated) last week. Since we are fully vaccinated, we don't have to wear masks as often. Some places still require masks, which I'm happy to do, but the virus in not gone. The last time I looked, there had been more than 33 million reported cases of the virus in the U.S. and 601,000 deaths. One of those will live in my heart forever. New cases are very low in our area, but southern Missouri is the current epicenter of new cases and hospitalizations. That's probably because their vaccination rate is so low. President Biden had declared that his goal was to have 70 percent of all Americans vaccinated by July 4. We've fallen far short of that, not from lack of effort or availability but from lack of faith in the vaccine or fear of the vaccine—I'm not sure which. I'm just glad to have received the vaccine and to feel free to go out without fear of the virus. However, I fear that with such a low vaccine rate, the virus will return with a vengeance. Only time will tell.

All sorts of shortages related in one way or another to the global pandemic still exist. Lumber is nearly impossible to get, as are many other building supplies. The pandemic closed factories in the U.S. but also in China. Supplies of all sorts of things from China are way behind schedule. Even Detroit is having trouble producing cars without parts from China. But we've learned to live with shortages. At least there's plenty of toilet paper. The 2020 Tokyo Olympics will be held this month (in 2021, but they kept "2020" in the official name). Spectators are not allowed, not even family members, so even if Jonas Travel were still in business, we would have no clients going. We'll all just be watching the Games on TV.

We've also made real vacation plans. We've rented a house in Destin, Florida, in August. We're not quite ready for a hotel yet—there's still too much infection around—but it is a vacation on a beach. I'm so excited. I'll probably cook most of our meals—something that would have given me shivers a year and a half ago. But I'm perfectly fine with it now. It's a little "safer" and cheaper. Finances still remain an issue, but it's getting better. We've learned to live on a budget. It's not such a bad thing. My mother will be moving into her new condo this fall. She will be going to Florida with us. Daisy will stay with Korie's family. I wish they could go with us, but they couldn't get the time off. Since Nathan and I both work virtually, it's much easier to pick up and go. Nathan doesn't think his company will ever go back to working in the office full-time. His company actually sold some of its office space, which makes going back nearly impossible. We've adjusted to that too. When my mother moves, we'll make her room into an office for me. Nathan will keep his larger office. Our future looks bright. Very different, but bright. We are different people now. Better, I think. Poorer in material ways but richer in other, more important, ways. I don't know what the world will bring our way next. I don't know when we will see the end to this awful pandemic, but whatever comes, we will be able to face it.

My greatest joy in the last four months was the day after we were fully vaccinated when we entered Pathways Church for a Sunday service. All five of us (Mom included) dressed in our Sunday best and walked into this simple but elegant church. We've been watching online for so long, it felt like coming home. Over the door was their motto: "Bringing together imperfect people in pursuit of a whole life." I squeezed Nathan's hand when I saw it. I noticed he'd been reading it too. "That's so us," I said with a smile. He smiled back. Our kids went to Sunday School for the first time. My mother is thinking of signing up to teach. We felt home. Loved. Connected to God. At the end of the service, the pastor read a prayer that summed up how much I've gained and learned in My Lost Year:

"Lord, open my eyes to the gifts you lay before me every day. Help me to understand that despite the misfortune and tragedy I sometimes face, blessings are everywhere, and challenges are often gifts in disguise. May I learn to trust that in all circumstances you are with me in ways far beyond my imagining, and that in you there is hope. May I learn to see that all I am and all I have is a gift from you. Let me be thankful for that gift and may I have the courage to share it with others. Help me to live my life as a reflection of your love and generosity with gratitude for today and hope for tomorrow. Amen."

# About the Author

Carin Fahr Shulusky was born and raised in west St. Louis County. She attended the University of Missouri, Columbia, where she received a B.J. (Bachelor of Journalism). After college she worked in advertising for GE and Monsanto. She was the first professional woman in her division at each company.

After 25 years in Marketing, she created her own firm, Marketing Alliance, where she was president from 2002-2014. She is a past-president of the Business Marketing Association of St. Louis.

Carin Fahr is married to Richard Shulusky. They have two grown children and one marvelous granddaughter. Grandma Carin has a life-long love of cooking, even writing her own cookbook.

In 2014 Carin retired to devote full time to writing. Her first book, *In the Middle,* was inspired by her own battle to care for her beloved mother, Dorothy Fahr. Many of the stories Carrie Young's mother tells her in *In the Middle* came from Carin's mother.

Carin is a lifelong member of Pathfinder Church in Ellisville, Missouri, where she volunteers in early childhood. She is on the board of the Special Education Foundation for St. Louis County.